LOST MAGIC

The Fated Kingdoms

Book One

E. J. MATTER

*For anyone who has ever wanted to curl up in the pages of a book
and make themselves at home.*

PROLOGUE

Beyond the reality of this world, in another realm were two kingdoms intertwined by love, curiosity, and greed. The kingdom of Mearan was filled with magic and wonder, while Westrim was full of knowledge and courage. For a time, peace flowed between the two kingdoms as the people lived amongst one another. Each kingdom drew from the other, providing a perfect balance of magic and knowledge.

Many found joy in the magic. They welcomed the miracle of it. And those from Mearan, the kingdom of magic, sought the knowledge of Westrim and the stability that came from it. The people learned how each kingdom lived, and with understanding and seeing, friendships grew, and from those friendships, sometimes, love.

As their curiosity and understanding grew, so did their desire for what they didn't have. Some in Westrim coveted the magic that they couldn't wield themselves. They became corrupt with their desire for it. As it was, many in Mearan were envious of Westrim's vast knowledge and craved it, for they understood it to be its own elevated form of power. While love and happiness are powerful emotions, so are jealousy and greed. These are consuming emotions that overtake the mind and invade the heart. Feelings that steal your good sense and can lead you blindly to your deepest desires or greatest disappointments. They can lead to peace... or war.

Despite the conspirators in each kingdom, many stayed loyal to the peaceful reign of the two kingdoms. They forged bonds and continued to live amongst one another without incident. Until it came about when the balance that was so evenly yoked tipped.

Differences that were once celebrated were now seen as a threat. The distrust between the two kingdoms grew with each passing day. Both sides silently and secretly gathered their forces and prepared for the worst. No one wanted to take the first step until an illness spread like wildfire throughout Westrim. Despite the extensive knowledge and considerable abilities at their disposal, no one could provide answers about the disease that seemed to have no plausible origin. Without any logical cause, the already shaky foundation between the kingdoms crumbled as minds turned to the one thing that wasn't rational: magic.

Westrim's King and Queen sent messengers to the surrounding regions and asked for help from anyone who could provide answers. Their pleas were met with silence. Without a forthcoming reply, they believed that the magical kingdom of Mearan had conjured the mysterious illness that claimed the lives of many, including, in time, the King and Queen themselves. The people demanded justice for the affliction brought upon their own.

Because of the extent of the silent, insidious unrest that had sprung up between the two kingdoms, Mearan believed that the illness was used as a self-sacrificial plan of Westrim.

If that was the case, it was a plot to gain sympathizers from other regions to advance Westrim's numbers in their burgeoning cause to vanquish the magic.

In a bid to put the dissention to rest once and for all, Westrim utilized every ounce of intelligence and information at their disposal and borrowed magic from an accomplice to set a plot in motion. Because Mearan couldn't stop what was coming, they had to protect what they could. By using the knowledge of Westrim from those loyal to them, they were assisted in devising a spell for their protection, a plan that had a built-in failsafe for what was to come. As fate would have it, even when torn apart, the conflicting sides sought opposing counsel. Ultimately, they needed each other to determine their futures and their fates.

To give themselves their best chance, Mearan was left almost entirely powerless and trapped within the safety of their kingdom. They hid the magic and locked it safely away from even themselves until the time fate destined for its release, if and when certain conditions were met. To release it would take more than a key, as something much more substantial than a lock protects it.

It waits for the one who will come back and awaken it. One who possesses magic and knowledge, and only has to find the courage in themselves to bring back the wonder and restore peace once again.

CHAPTER ONE

Hooves that matched the rhythm of her heart thundered on the ground. The horse beneath her trotted through the path in the forest with speed and grace. But when the forest met the clearing, the animal broke free into a gallop. Its rider lifted her face to the sun's warm caress and closed her eyes. The scent of the field's flowers and the horse surrounded her as the cool air filled her lungs. Ellery Faidman found joy in moments like these, and peace, a feeling that was often elusive.

Too soon, the gallop slowed down to a trot as they crested a hill on the other side of the grassy clearing. Ellery opened her eyes and looked down the hill. A breath caught in her chest at the sight of a castle in the distance.

"How beautiful," she breathed out, a smile on her pretty face.

The castle was framed by golden-hued rolling hills and a cloudless blue sky. Its pointed sharp towers were so tall it seemed like they could reach up and touch the sun. The spires bore little shingles that looked like scales, protective and strong.

The sun's glare made the castle's milky white exterior look like it was glowing. Gold adorned the towers' tips and trimmed the ledges and windows of the castle, giving it a bold touch of grandeur.

Its windows were the only thing that shone brighter than its white and gold exterior. The way the sun cast its bright light on the stained-glass windows caused a spectrum of colors and shapes to reflect upon the surrounding area.

Enchanting. That's how Ellery would describe it, if asked.

It looked like it was from a fairy tale. Something about it pulled at her. She wanted to explore within its majestic walls and discover the secrets held in the kingdom surrounding it.

She wondered who lived there, in that picturesque castle. The thought seemed to latch onto her mind and filled her with the oddest feeling. A wave of urgency flooded her, but she wasn't sure why… or for what.

She felt so close to the answer that it almost pained her. It was as if the castle's purpose was right on the tip of her mind. But each time she tried to focus on it, its meaning managed to slip away.

She had been to this spot before and each time had the same sense of knowing deep inside her bones. It was a feeling surreal and yet familiar. This sense of knowing made her feel as if she was connected to something greater than herself, as if time and space were intertwined in ways that could not be explained by mere words alone and had brought her to that moment. No matter how hard she tried to shake off the urgency, the knowing, the emotions, kept coming back stronger each time until finally, they consumed her entirely.

And that was when she woke up.

Ellery sat straight up in bed and tried to breathe through thoughts that were too much to comprehend, and too strong to ignore before laying her head between her drawn-up knees, trying desperately to find her equilibrium.

On the night of her twenty-first birthday, she began to have dreams unlike any she had ever experienced. They left her breathless, filled with a need to *go* and *do*. For months she had visited a place full of wonder and beauty, where she explored up until that very point where she'd always awaken, wanting more. As each night passed by, her dreams became clearer and more vivid as she saw a land full of lush green hills rising far into the horizon, sparkling rivers meandering through forests, and richly colored flowers. But then, she would wake up before she was able to ride her horse to the castle.

She was consumed by the peacefulness that filled her when she was there, the feeling as if time had stopped and all that mattered was being… living… breathing. There was urgency, too. But she could not explain why. Each dream held awareness, haunting her daily thoughts, making her wonder what the dreams meant. The relentless dreams clung to her even when she was awake. There was no escape. She dreamt of people she had never met that belonged to lands that were not her own.

Her breath caught each time she thought of him. The man of her dreams, the one whose presence pulled at her. Even in dreams she felt a connection to him. Seeing him felt like destiny was calling to her. With a smile, she closed her eyes and beckoned a picture of him to the forefront of her mind. The way his sandy blonde hair was tousled and wavy atop a face chiseled and elegant. His friendly light gray eyes were framed by thick lashes and never looked anything less than intelligent and intense. Ellery blushed thinking of his full lips… and all the things she wanted them to do to her. She sighed dreamily. He was the kind of handsome that made you stop and stare for just a moment longer than necessary.

In her dreams he never failed to carry himself with a quiet confidence that attracted her to him. He had an air of mystery about him, like he was hiding something, and she desperately wanted to know what his secrets were.

He was always alone, standing apart from everyone else. In this he reminded her of herself. Maybe that explained why she felt such a strong pull toward him. But the more she saw him in her dreams, the more she thought of him in each waking hour. It was as if she was tethered to the dreams because of her desire to know him. She lay in bed that morning with this feeling, while her mind was telling her it was something far greater than that which pulled her into her dreams at night. Each morning when she awoke, she felt she had lost something. She ached for something or someone unnamed that was missing. Something just out of reach.

Ellery shook off her thoughts and, with a start, looked at the clock on the wall. She realized she had slept through her alarm.

"Oh crap! I can't be late," she announced to herself.

She dressed quickly and ran to the bathroom to get ready. She stood before the mirror in the bathroom and lifted her head.

"I will figure this out. One of these nights I'll stay longer in my dream and I'll…" She paused there. What would she do? She shrugged. "I'll figure that part out, too."

Her gaze moved back to the mirror. Her dark brown hair mimicked her restless spirit, never willing to settle on bouncing into curls or staying entirely straight, but the wild waves suited her. She usually thought of herself as average, at least physically, but when she saw herself, she saw that dogged determination that helped her survive foster care and ace her college classes.

Full of antsy energy, she wished she had time for a jog to clear her mind. Jogging was the only thing she could depend on to outrace her runaway mind that always seemed to be flitting from topic to topic. It also helped to keep her body toned. She had long, lean legs and a slim waist because of it, but luckily the long bouts of cardio didn't take away her curves. She enjoyed them, but instead of playing into her best physical features that day, she threw on the nearest outfit and reached up to pull her long hair back into a ponytail.

Do I take after my mom… or my dad? I guess I'll never know.

She'd long since stopped asking for details about her birth parents. Focusing on the future seemed more promising than digging up the past. She sighed when she took in her appearance, tired hazel eyes looked back at her. She was paler than usual, which was something to say because she was fair to begin with, and it made her light smattering of freckles stick out even more. She decided her appearance was as good as it was going to get today and walked out of the bathroom to forage for a cup of coffee and a protein bar to take to class.

CHAPTER TWO

Ellery loved learning, and she found use for each new piece of knowledge that was given to her. With her usual energy she breezed into the university's lecture hall, putting thoughts of her dream in the back of her mind. The chaotic noises of the students chatting and shuffling through their belongings as they prepared for class filled the large, open space. As she pulled out her laptop and notebook from her bag, there was a tingling at the base of her neck. A sudden awareness of the energy around her settled over her, making its way from her neck down to the palms of her hands. She could almost see the energy around her. It called to her. Then, as quickly as it had come, it was gone, leaving a lingering sense of unease in its wake.

She rubbed her hands together, noting how warm they were, and looked around. Out of the corner of her eye she caught a glimpse of tousled blonde hair.

Is it him? Is he here? Her breath caught in her throat as a wave of attraction rushed through her.

She studied the blonde locks carefully, her heart pounding. She would know that hair anywhere. It had to be him—the man in her dreams who had woven a spell on her thoughts since the first moment she laid eyes on him. She inhaled sharply as the tingling sensation from just moments ago now returned and filled her body.

She couldn't stop the smile of delight from forming on her slender face. This gorgeous man had somehow walked out of a dream and into reality—her reality! The reality of how close he was to her broke through her reverie, and she saw his head turn as he glanced toward her. When those soft gray eyes fell on her, the gold flecks in them playing off of the blonde of his hair, her heart constricted. She felt the intensity of his gaze as if it were touching her skin, sending a shock through her. For a second, she was frozen in place, but that was overshadowed by the fear that he would vanish back into dreamland. Impulsively she rose to her feet and her chair fell back and clattered onto the floor behind her.

The sudden loud noise reverberated throughout the hall, making many of her classmates jump in surprise. Even the professor seemed to be momentarily taken aback, leaning forward to see if she was okay. All eyes turned towards her. She closed her own eyes and took a deep breath, trying to quell the racing of her heart. When she opened them and let the world around her come into focus, a sinking feeling filled her chest. The man before her wasn't him. The eyes that looked back at her weren't the beautiful gray she imagined they were. They were a pretty shade of blue. Instead of tousled blonde hair it was clipped short military style, and he had a sweet, boyish face. A handsome young man, but not hers.

"Are you okay?" he asked a bit uncertainly.

He looked at her with concern, and although he had stood up, he had not taken a step toward her. She could only imagine the crazed look in her eyes that made him stop in his tracks. At his words her cheeks flushed as she leaned down to pick up the chair.

"Yes, thanks. Too much caffeine this morning." Ellery offered him a rueful smile, feeling her cheeks flame crimson from embarrassment. A few of her classmates nodded in understanding before everyone went back to their conversations.

She sat back down, starting to seriously doubt if it was advisable to think about her dreams when she was awake. She reminded herself it was the caffeine and the lack of restful sleep as she tried to make sense of the rushing sensation that still surged through her body. She felt like something deep within her was being drawn out, and she couldn't control it. She forced herself to calm down by silently counting to ten three times, and when she did, the waves of unsettling sensations inside of her receded.

She was starting to question her own sanity. The dreams were getting more intense with each passing night, taking a toll on her. Even now, she felt remnants of them tugging at her consciousness, the weight of them like an anchor dragging her down.

The rest of the class was a blur. She tried to focus on the professor's words, but it was useless. Each minute seemed to drag on, and visions of her dreams teased her at the edges of her mind. When she finally left the hall and walked outside, she felt a weight settle on her shoulders. She knew that no matter how she tried to justify it away, the energy she'd felt flooding her body was special, and it was getting stronger after each nightly dream.

~ ~ ~

Ellery sat at the library's service desk, a central station on the first floor. She slumped a bit in the swivel chair, eyeing the dated computer before her. Sticky notes were scattered along the high back of the library's service desk, most faded with time. Heat emanated comfortably from the computer's tower tucked on the floor under the desk.

This is real, she assured herself. *This is safe. No more seeing or feeling things today.*

She scanned the room, looking for something to do to take her mind off her relentless memories of her dreams. If she spun the chair around, she could see most of the two-story library all at once. She was there to advise and support those who came to hide away from the demands of life in a book or use the library's resources.

"Focus on the job, and you'll be fine," she muttered softly.

Almost seeing the man in her dreams today had shaken her deeply. She hadn't known just how deeply she was connected to him. Normally, Ellery was tough, strong enough to forge through life with little support. Warmth teased her heart as his face came to her mind again. Would she be haunted by this yearning for him forever?

She got to her feet and pretended to organize the notes, documents, and mismatched pens strewn across the resource desk. She needed to find something to do to forget about him.

She heard chairs scraping against the floor as they were pulled out from a table and soft greetings from one human to another. It brought her back to the present moment, and she checked the time on her phone. Her eyes bulged out of her head. Was it already almost the end of her shift? She must have daydreamed through most of it, unless she was in some sort of time warp.

A familiar whistling sound greeted her. She looked up to her see her coworker, Lily, walking in. Ellery smiled when she saw the large stack of books Lily was carrying. When Lily got closer, she smiled her wide grin back at Ellery over the tower of books.

"Excuse me, miss, but we aren't allowed to make loud noises in the library," Ellery teased.

Lily guffawed in her buoyant, rebellious way. "Good thing I work here, so I won't be kicking myself out any time soon."

Ellery had always thought her friend was gorgeous, based not just on her looks but also confirmed by the endless supply of attention she attracted everywhere she went. Carefully manicured brows hung over heavily made up eyes that would have looked pretentious on anyone else. The smokey shadow and thick liner only drew out the depths of her caramel-colored eyes which were beautiful against Lily's warm copper skin. Her curly dark hair bounced with each authoritative step. She was the epitome of effortlessly glamorous, with a body shape to match.

Ellery often wondered why the only men Lily ever talked about were in the books she read. She was spunky, playful, and opinionated. Even to Ellery, the constant loner, Lily's energy was infectious without feeling overwhelming. Lily commanded attention without even trying, and she knew it.

Ellery sprang to her feet to help Lily as the pile of books started to topple over. Lily might have only been a few inches shorter than her own 5'4", but it seemed like Ellery was comparatively a giant when it came to anything physical like lugging books around.

"Thank you!" Lily exclaimed. "I should have made two trips, but I didn't want to be late for my shift. I was already pushing time due to a beautiful prince. I've been courting him in my mind for days." She tilted her head toward the young adult section. "My latest fantasy is courtesy of the new young adult book that just came in." She looked down at one of the covers of the books in her hands, stroking the bare torso of a muscled hero. "These men, I swear. They make dating a real guy so disappointing!"

Ellery waggled her eyebrows. "Oh, it's that good?"

"Yep! So, it's about a girl. Every night instead of the dreams normal people have, the heroine ends up in another world. She doesn't find out until later that her dreams are actually real!" She paused and sighed dramatically. "So cool. Anyway, she wants to go home at first, to get the heck out of the dream world, but something changes her mind. Can you guess?" she asked, and her caramel eyes flickered playfully. Ellery tugged the book from the counter and clutched it to her chest.

"The love interest showed up, of course. I don't blame her. I wouldn't be afraid of heading there either, if that was what was waiting for me. Melatonin and a strict bedtime would be my new best friends."

"Interesting," Ellery said, only hearing half of what Lily was saying over the pounding in her head. What would have been even more interesting was the look on Lily's face as she stared at Ellery waiting for her reaction, but Ellery missed this because she was off in her own world and trying not to panic. Her hands grew warm and tingly.

"So, that is what has you all a flutter today?" Ellery finally said casually, masking her feelings like a pro. Growing up without knowing where she was from or who her parents were had taught her how to pretend all was well, even if it wasn't.

"Wouldn't gray eyes, blonde hair, and four percent body fat do it for you, too?" Lily teased, her eyes studying Ellery.

Ellery coughed and reached for her steel water bottle. After a long drink she fixed her hazel eyes on her friend. The perfect description of the man in her dreams made her pause, but she covered that up with a simple, "I prefer brunettes."

Ellery escaped further discomfort by noting the time and going to clock out.

"Liar," Lily called out after her with a laugh.

Ellery gave her a smile over her shoulder and waved goodbye.

Once out of sight, her fake smile dropped. Lily's description of that book—it was her experience exactly! Could it possibly be a coincidence? She wasn't sure of anything anymore. She was determined to go home, make some hot chocolate, and reread one of her favorite books. That should calm down her befuddled thoughts.

This day could not end fast enough. But even then, there was no peace for her when dreaming, either.

CHAPTER THREE

Ellery walked into her brick apartment building and headed for the stairs to clomp her way to the second floor. When she reached the landing she paused, cocking her head to listen. Strains of classical music drifted through the air of the hallway. Its unfamiliar notes mesmerized her as they echoed off the walls and invited her to draw closer.

I must go there, her mind told her. *I must go!* The thought was more urgent now.

She felt her feet move of their own accord. Her confusion turned to alarm when she realized that the soothing melody was coming from her apartment. Her supposedly *empty* apartment. How had someone gotten in?

She should have called 911 but her temper flared. She'd never had a proper home, and her apartment was her safe place, the home she'd created for herself. Her hands balled into little fists, and despite every reason not to, she still felt herself pushing through the energy she could almost see, set on her doorway.

Before she could follow her instincts and take another step, she shrieked as she felt a hand on her shoulder.

"I'm armed!" she lied, whirling around to face the person.

"That's good, dearie. A girl as pretty as you, living alone, should be armed."

Ellery let out a strained laugh, placing a hand over her rapidly beating heart. "Mrs. Hansen! You scared me half to death."

Ellery looked into the kind eyes of her elderly neighbor. They were a rich, dark blue with creases of a life well-lived at the corners. Her expertly dyed hair was a honey blonde with dark undertones. It was short and tidy, which is what Ellery thought of when she thought of Mrs. Hansen—perfectly styled and neat as a pin. She never had a hair out of place. The sight of her familiar face smiling immediately set Ellery at ease.

The smile on Mrs. Hansen's face quickly turned to a look full of concern. "Is everything okay, dearie?" The gentle tone was tinged with worry as her eyes, sharp as a whip, quickly scanned the younger woman, as if looking for something. Satisfied, the older woman hmphed and patted Ellery's arm.

"Yes, Mrs. Hansen. Everything is fine," she said trying so hard to act normally. But after a day of pretending, she was exhausted. "I just… I thought I heard a noise coming from inside my apartment." She needed to get it together. She was sure she'd spooked everyone around her that day.

Mrs. Hansen slightly inclined her head toward Ellery's door and shook her head. Ellery waited for her neighbor to hear the music, to verify that she wasn't going crazy. "I don't hear anything now. Do you want me to wait and go in with you?"

Awesome, Ellery thought to herself. *Crazy it is.*

"Um, no. It was just my phone playing music. It must have bumped something in my pocket. Have a great night," Ellery squeaked out, eager to retreat into her apartment, intruder or no intruder.

Mrs. Hansen nodded slowly, her sharp blue eyes boring into Ellery's. Ellery could tell she wasn't entirely sure she should leave her, but the woman turned to walk across the hall. "I'm right across the hall if you need anything."

Ellery nodded in thanks and took her time finding the keys in her purse, not wanting Mrs. Hansen to still be in the hallway when she opened the door. When Ellery heard the click of the door across from her latching shut, she grabbed the keys that she had been holding onto with a vise-like grip. With a shaky hand she turned the key in the lock.

Her jaw dropped and her mouth hung agape before she promptly slammed the door in her own face.

This damn day, she thought to herself.

Never one to run from a challenge, she mentally prepared for what was coming next. Then she straightened her back and opened the door. Shock, curiosity, and no small amount of hidden fear flooded her as her eyes darted around the room.

"What on earth?" She laughed nervously, in shock.

Instead of her apartment, her eyes met with a ballroom, one that, after a moment, she recognized as the one she had visited before in her dreams. It was just like one of her dreams, yet so vivid and lifelike that it felt real, like she would be swept up in the merriment of the ballroom that was right before her. Her eyes chased after the dozens of details in front of her. She closed the door behind her, committing herself to the moment, no matter the cost.

She couldn't help but nervously laugh again at the absurdity of it all. She was sure that the harsh laugh that came out of her had turned into one that sounded slightly maniacal. Not that the couples gracing the dance floor in the middle of the beautiful ballroom before her noticed the crazy hazel-eyed woman cackling on the edge of the dance floor. She was surprised she wasn't mistaken as some old-time witch from centuries gone by.

Her laughs turned into anxiety, and for a minute she gasped for air. "You've got this," she said to herself. "Don't act like a madwoman in front of your guests." That ridiculous thought threatened to bring the crazed laughter back. But before it did, she forced herself to take a step inside.

She looked toward the dance floor, and the music became hauntingly slow and beautiful. Couples moved in perfect harmony, spinning around the floor with ease and grace and for a moment she wished she was one of them. She scanned the dancers and saw that glint of blonde hair in the light. Like earlier, her breath caught, and she started shuffling left and right to try and get a look at his face, but he was lost in the sea of dancers. Then she saw it again, and her chest tightened. This was her moment. He was here, and she was coming for him. She took a step forward as the song reached its crescendo and then, the music faded away, along with the rest of the room. She found herself alone in the middle of her studio apartment.

A wave of emotions flowed through her body, a flurry of confusion, excitement, and fear. Not being able to settle on just one feeling, Ellery focused on taking a few deep breaths and then moved to sit down on one of the barstools at her kitchen island. She shook her head slowly and looked around to make sure her apartment was still her apartment. As with most studios, it had one main living space, with doors belonging only to the bathroom and a small closet, so it was safe to say as she took it in with one sweep that it was hers again.

"Mine again," she muttered, rubbing her arms with her hands. "Alone."

She suddenly missed the bright, happy faces of the dancing couples. She missed his face. He was so close, and then it all just vanished.

"I'm going to figure this out," she vowed to herself.

And she knew one way to do it. She'd document everything she'd been dreaming, and everything she saw here tonight. Then, she'd piece it all together, bit by bit. She could even use it for her thesis for her MFA program. She walked toward her desk and pulled out a fresh notebook, brows furrowed in thought. She opened it up to a fresh page and began to write, feverishly, as if her life depended on documenting each detail.

She thought of the meadow she had dreamed of a few nights before, and the peace she had felt there. She thought of the castle, and the horse she was riding. Everything she captured in words.

The emotionally trying day was finally catching up to her, and her eyes began to droop, but she couldn't stop yet. The details came easier when she settled her mind and let them come. She was tired and relaxed and allowed each dream to flood her mind. She wrote until she drifted off to sleep.

CHAPTER FOUR

There were a few places where Ellery usually woke up, none of which were outside her studio apartment. In bed, like a normal person, or in her chair, if she fell asleep reading, or at her desk working where the keyboard served as her pillow. The latter must have happened because she was incredibly stiff as she woke up. She kept her eyes closed for another few seconds until she realized not only was she not sitting up, but she could feel warmth on her face. She pushed herself up, and the minute her fingers made contact with what should have been her bed, her eyes flew open in a panic. She would have screamed, but fear stole her breath and panic became rooted deep in her chest.

She looked around frantically and realized she was outside. She tried to stand up, but dizziness and a swift wave of nausea washed over her. She knelt down on shaky hands and knees and let her hands dig into the grass.

Is this real?

Despite the fear threatening to suffocate her, she stood and gathered enough courage to look around. When she did, the first layer of terror and fear eased as she recognized the place she was standing in. She had been writing about it right before she fell asleep. Once her heartbeat had steadied, and she was able to look more clearly without panic clouding her mind, she saw that the meadow had its first taste of fall. Okay, so wherever she was, it was the same season as home, saying goodbye to summer and heading into fall. While some flowers still held their color, others were turning brown, drying up, and dying along with the end of the season. The sun shone brightly, its rays dappling the grass with a golden light. A forest on one side of the field had a river running alongside it. It wasn't city air either that she was breathing in, it was fresh and clean, just like in her dreams.

"This can't be real. I must be dreaming." She realized this with an almost painful relief.

Although in dreams she had always been entitled to the awareness of knowing it was just that, a dream. There was a surety in knowing that. There was no such feeling now. Maybe she was having some sort of out-of-body experience. She looked to see if anyone was around before she closed her eyes and did a little hop in place. Although she wasn't sure if the jump was to verify that the ground was firm beneath her or if when her feet touched, she would somehow be standing on the stained wood floor in her apartment.

When she thought of her apartment, Mrs. Hansen and the strange way that Ellery had acted the last time that nice old lady saw her came to mind. She couldn't imagine what Mrs. Hansen would tell the authorities when they showed up after she missed a few shifts at work. That she had been acting a bit off, she was a bit of a loner, nice enough, but troubled…? She would be written off, of that Ellery was sure.

Ellery looked at the water sparkling in the distance and wanted to walk over to it.

"The ground is real, and if the water is real, too, then I've got a big problem on my hands." And that problem was, how to get out of this dream that didn't feel like a dream.

If she allowed herself to believe this was real, there was no going back. She focused on the sun beating off the water and the current's small movements and ripples. She couldn't stand in one spot forever. She took a tentative first step as if the ground was going to crumble and she would go down an endless hole. Since she didn't sink, she released the breath she didn't know she was holding. She reached the river with its huge rocky ledges along the shoreline and peered toward the water as if it held the answers to her burning questions.

She felt the urge to touch it, to feel the coolness against her hand. It looked the same as any other river. As believable as it was, and even though she could feel the ground beneath her feet, she reached down to touch it, to feel it against her hand for confirmation.

~ ~ ~

Alexei Sonders was headed toward the forest. This was his last foray as a free man, able to mostly do what he pleased. From the time he was young, he knew the expectations set for him and what would be required with a bloodline like his. He took his responsibilities seriously, was self-disciplined, worked hard, and had spent his entire life living up to the demanding standards set for him. It was all the more reason for his little excursion to be considered reckless, but for once, he didn't care. Changes were coming, big ones, whether he was ready or not.

He reached the edge of a meadow and without warning the ground shook, as a shimmering wind swirled like a funnel in the middle of the clearing. Before he could steady himself, the wind shot out of the funnel in all directions like it was going to level everything around it. It looked like a giant curtain that was heading his way. He felt it as the wind crashed into him, whipped through him, and then vanished like it never happened. Immediately, the sun was shining and the birds were chirping.

"What the hell was that?" he murmured to himself.

He waited a few minutes, watchful for danger before going to investigate. He saw movement. He watched as a woman sat up. He saw emotion flash across her face. He wasn't close enough to see everything, but shock, confusion, and panic he could see well enough. Especially the latter, because the panic was practically radiating off of her in waves.

From a distance, he could see her alluring beauty and the features of her face that were lovely. Her dark brown hair was casually pulled back but ready to fall out of its binding. His fingers itched at the thought of wanting to get his hands in it shining as the sun beat down on it. He also took note of her outfit and the stark contrast to what he was accustomed to see women in. He quickly realized that this girl was not like most women. There was something about her that he couldn't quite put his finger on, but it drew him in with a hunger.

Her clothing was different. He didn't recognize the jacket's fabric, but the shirt underneath seemed to be black and plain. When she stood he realized that the pants were a whole other matter altogether. He couldn't help himself when his mouth seemed to go dry. The pants were dark, like indigo, tight enough that they showed off the curve of her hips and were tightly molded against her legs. Legs that he couldn't help but observe were long and lean. He could see the muscles flexing when she moved.

He watched as she hopped in place, and all that beautiful brown hair bounced around her. Afterward, she peeked, ever so slightly, out of one opened eye. He was charmed beyond reason. Briefly, he wondered where she came from and if he could follow her if she went back. Before he allowed himself to really think about how to approach her, he watched as she walked toward the river.

Since it didn't seem like she was in a rush, he figured he would take another minute to figure out his course of action. If he moved too obviously, she would bolt, and he wanted, needed, to meet her. As he watched he realized that she was so intent on the water that she wasn't paying attention to her footing and was going to fall in. Her foot that was on the edge of a rock started to slip, and he ran.

One second, Ellery started falling toward the sparkling water and the next, she was pulled back against a hard, warm surface that rose and fell in steady breaths. She leaned back for a moment, weak at the knees at the fact that she almost went down headfirst into the fast-flowing water. She felt safe and steady against the warmth behind her. She breathed in the smells of pine and grass… and something musky. She wasn't sure how long it took her to realize that someone had pulled her up and held her back against their chest. All at once she could feel the heat spreading from their body to hers. She felt their breathing more acutely.

"It's okay. You are safe," a low voice whispered in her ear, and she felt his warm breath on her cheek.

She froze, her weak knees instantly becoming steel rods. When she tensed it arched her back further into the muscled chest behind her. The arm around her waist tightened protectively and her breath quickened.

She turned in the circle of his arms and was prepared to bolt, but when she saw his face, her feet were glued to the ground.

It's him!

He towered over her in both height and build as she looked up into the handsome face that she had seen so many times before in her dreams. Except this time, she was touching him, so he had to be real. Blonde hair fell over his forehead as he looked down at her with eyes the color of gray morning mist. Her chest heaved as her heart raced. Being in his arms felt so good… so right.

I've been waiting for you for such a long time, she thought, her eyes latched on his.

She felt as if she couldn't think straight as emotions fluttered inside of her. She couldn't help but stare at the face she had seen so many times, a face that seemed as if it was sculpted by desire itself. She wanted to trace her finger over the high places of his cheekbones and trail it down to lips that were so soft and full, made for whispered promises and stolen kisses. His eyes dropped to her own lips, but he clenched his jaw and raked his gaze back to meet hers.

He was her dreams come to life, like her heart and mind had manifested him. She couldn't help but trail her eyes over the rest of him. She started at his broad shoulders and allowed herself to journey down over his muscled arms which seemed to be fighting the constraints of the thin shirt he had folded up to his elbows. The rest of him was long and lean, and she briefly wondered what he did to achieve those taut muscles. She felt her cheeks turn a shade of pink as she took each well-defined muscle in. She swallowed hard trying to find her voice, unable to look away as her gaze swept over him. She frowned as he casually took his hands from her waist and put them in his pockets. She wanted more of this man.

With effort she raised her eyes to his. His light eyes looked translucent in the sunlight allowing them to flick nearly undetected down her body, her curves, taking in each one. When his eyes moved back up to hers, a smile tugged at the corner of his lips—inviting, so inviting. And something more. She saw in his depths the confidence of a leader, a man used to holding the weight of the world on his shoulders, which made her a little jealous of the world, she wanted him to hold her too.

She waited to see recognition flicker in those eyes as he looked at her, but it never came. And she was certain of one thing, he had never seen her before. But the really interesting part was that if he was surprised that she was standing there so obviously out of place, he didn't let on. Instead, he looked intrigued.

"Are you okay?" he finally asked, at least she was pretty sure that was what he asked.

She was having a hard time listening to anything he was saying when her head was still spinning with the reality that he was standing so close to her. She heard that his voice was soft and comforting and nodded absently.

"I'm Alexei."

She let the name roll around in her head, putting a name with the face she had become so familiar with. He looked at her expectantly, waiting for her to reciprocate.

"Ellery," she said before she could think better of it. She didn't know quite where she was, so maybe she shouldn't give out her real identity.

"And where are you going on this pretty fall day, Ellery?"

"Crazy," she muttered under her breath. That was exactly where she was going if she continued to let herself believe any of this was real.

"Where?" he asked as if he hadn't heard her but the smirk on his face told her otherwise.

She could lie and say she was just out for a walk, or heading to a friend's house, but she thought of herself, how she looked, how she spoke, what she wore—there was no possible way he would believe that. Instead, she shrugged her shoulders, and that was as honest as she could get.

He nodded as if that was the answer he had expected. "In that case, I am taking a holiday at a friend's cabin for the next few days," he said slowly and carefully, measuring his words. "It is a few hours walk from here." He nodded toward the forest. "You are more than welcome to come with me until you ..." he paused, "figure things out."

Of course, her inner self practically rolled her eyes. Why wouldn't he be staying in the middle of the forest. That wasn't suspicious or anything. Although, she wasn't actually there anyway, right? It wasn't possible. She was in another vision, walking through another dream. So why not follow the handsome stranger deep into the woods to some remote cottage? She could simply go along with it until she woke up.

He began to shift his weight and looked around as if expecting someone to jump out from the bushes.

"Waiting for someone?" she asked pertly as she followed his gaze.

He looked at her in surprise, and then masked his face again. "No one important."

That piqued her interest and concern, and she said nothing, clearly not believing what he said.

"Maybe we can talk about this later. We will have plenty of time to ask questions on the way."

"How do I know you're not dangerous?" she asked and held her ground.

"How do I know you aren't?" he quipped back to her. They locked eyes in a silent challenge. There was a predatory look in his gaze as his eyes latched on hers. He seemed to think for a minute, and she wondered what would have come out of his mouth if he had said what he was thinking right away. "I can be," he finally admitted. Then a slow, sensual smile spread across his lips. "But not to you."

"Are you on the run or something?"

He took a casual stance and appeared relaxed, but she could tell he was anything but.

"What exactly are you asking?"

Naturally, she wasn't able to back down. "Are you on the run?" she said slowly as if enunciating the same words would help him understand. He leveled a stare at her. "From the law," she finished.

His jaw ticked, and she couldn't tell if he was irritated or amused despite himself. "Not exactly."

She could tell that she wasn't going to get any more out of him. She already knew what she was going to do and decided to get on with it. "I guess this is as good as it's going to get."

He gave her an incredulous look and then laughed. It was like he had never heard that phrase before. She figured she would need to give as much as she got when it came to questions and answers. Not to mention that when it came to the two of them, she had to admit she was the worse bet. She was surprised he was willing to take her. She also was smart enough to know that the next person who showed up wouldn't be as hospitable.

Ellery opened her mouth to agree to move on until her skeptical side decided not to play nice and instead said, "One more question." He looked resigned and inclined his head toward her. "Why?"

"Why what?" he asked, and she wasn't sure if he was goading her or if he knew.

"Why take me along?" What she couldn't tell him was that the reason she trusted him was that she'd seen him before in this dream world. That had to count for something. She knew that there was more to him than what he was sharing. Nobody was that easy-going to just pick up a stranger and bring them home.

His gaze seemed to bore into her, and it sent a strange thrill through her. "It seems it would be better for both of us if I kept you close until we figure out what is going on." At that point she had to concede. They were both well aware that she clearly didn't belong there, but once again her judgy alter ego just couldn't keep her mouth shut.

"I could be a serial killer. Or maybe I'm on the run too, a criminal on the loose." She let out a light laugh. "We would be like a modern-day Bonnie and Clyde." Then she remembered how that famous gangster couple's story ended and grimaced slightly before looking over to see him step closer toward her.

"Are you?" he asked and put two fingers under her chin to tip her face up to his. Her breath caught. "A killer," he whispered, and the side of his mouth tipped up as if he knew how his closeness was affecting her.

"No," she said a bit unsteady but bolstered herself, "but that doesn't mean that I don't have it in me to start."

"Duly noted," he said and cupped her chin before stepping back. "I'll sleep with one eye open."

She realized he was making fun of her and gave him a look that would have withered a lesser man.

"I'm going to go get my bags and we can get going." He started to walk in the opposite direction and then turned around and walked backwards, keeping his eyes on her again. "Wouldn't want to turn my back on you. Who knows what you are capable of."

She considered her favorite single-finger hand gesture as a retort but instead shook her head and huffed a sigh before turning to look out at the river. She looked at the sun and guessed from its location that they only had a few hours left of daylight and potential serial killer skills or not she didn't want to be in the forest in the dark.

He headed back toward her but didn't stop walking. "Are you coming, Bonnie?"

Although she was sure he had no idea who Bonnie or Clyde were, the teasing made her smile. Needing someone's help caused her to hesitate. But given the circumstances, it was something that she would need to embrace… for now. She was someone who was self-sufficient and very proud of it. But not prideful. She wouldn't last a day out here on her own. Because of that, and before she could question her sanity, she matched his steps and walked toward the forest beside him.

"I can carry one," she said and reached for one of his bags, wanting to help.

He looked her over and adjusted the weight of the packs across his shoulders. "They are heavy."

"I'm not fragile."

"No," he said as he looked at her. She seemed to be anything but fragile, so he shrugged and handed her the smaller of the two. "That certainly isn't how I would describe you."

"Oh. How would you describe me?"

He smiled slyly. "I'll let you know."

She slung the bag over her shoulder and grinned over at him.

"That's a good look on you," he quipped.

She looked down at the bag and its material. "Canvas?"

"No, your smile."

CHAPTER FIVE

Alexei couldn't stop thinking of the moment she had first laid her pretty eyes on him. Those hazel eyes had gone wide and were filled with the look you give a long-lost friend… or a past lover. She recognized him. That much he knew. He was sure he hadn't seen her before, he would have remembered such a beautiful face. When he held her, he felt a sudden jolt of electricity pass between them.

Hadn't he been looking for what came next? Hadn't he just given in to the restlessness that had been plaguing him and that brought him to her? Maybe she was what was next. There was more he wanted to ask but for now he decided not to press and let her keep her secrets as he certainly had some of his own. He understood the need for privacy more than most and was willing to give her that. For now.

Ellery distracted herself by looking around. The forest had a mystique that rivaled that of her new traveling companion. The sound of crunching leaves and the smell of crisp autumn air surrounded her. The sun shone through the canopy above.

Its golden light cast a warmth in the otherwise cool breeze of the forest and filled the forest floor with sporadic bits of light and shadows.

She found herself eager to explore what lay beyond the trees as she admired the beauty that surrounded them. Everywhere she looked was an endless array of colors decorating their path. Some of the leaves had turned to shades of amber and gold, interspersed with the dark greens of the forest. It was a captivating combination.

As they walked along, she felt a need to talk to him, but struggled to find the right words. She started to say something multiple times, and then couldn't bring herself to speak. She wondered what counted as appropriate conversation in this instance, then decided there wasn't anything normal about it so maybe the same rules didn't apply. And even though he looked at her as if she was a puzzle to be solved, he was giving her time and space, and she appreciated it. If the roles were reversed, she wasn't sure how patient she would be.

The whole situation still had her mind flip flopping between this being the greatest adventure of her life and her knowing that it might not be real and would be over all too soon. But she was worried that the longer she didn't talk, the more quickly he would fill in the blanks himself. Since she wasn't sure what his mind would come up with, she needed to provide some answers herself and control her own narrative. She hadn't been in a position of control since she woke up in this strange place. Not that this would give her full control by any means, but knowledge was power, and she imagined that he had questions. She wanted information from him as well. Maybe they could barter and trade in that for a while.

She cleared her throat and found her voice. "I want to thank you. Not just for finding me, but for bringing me along."

"My pleasure." He didn't want her to retreat back to her thoughts. Now that she was opening up, he wanted to keep her talking. But before he could ask a question, she beat him to it.

"Let's just assume we both know that this is odd and somehow put that thought aside. Where am I, exactly?"

"The kingdom of Westrim." He watched as shock streaked across her features, and she mouthed the name in silence before composing herself.

"Exactly like I thought, not on any map that I have seen. I somehow traveled to a place that seemingly doesn't exist in my world." She raised her hands, then let them drop. "If I try to be logical it isn't in the cards. That leaves options that my mind just can't accept."

She wanted to tell him about the dreams but decided to hold that back for now. To her, he felt like someone she'd known for a long time, but she knew he may hold suspicions in his mind about her. Unless he'd been dreaming about her, too, he'd have no reason to trust her.

She reminded herself that there was something more here, something more to him. And more to all of it. She couldn't explain it but since she woke up there, she had a sort of understanding, a knowing, maybe. It felt like some information that she was privy to was already calculated in her head and, more sporadically, sifting through the cracks. Because of that she would trust her instincts.

He nodded. "I assumed as much. The part about you not being from here," he clarified, "but I appreciate you telling me."

"It was pretty lucky how you came along like you did. I almost faceplanted. Not a good look," Ellery said, making Alexei chuckle. "So, how did you find me?"

It was an innocent question he knew, but he wasn't sure how to answer it. It was his turn to withhold a piece of information as he assumed she had been doing as well. Why he was there and what he was doing wasn't something he was willing to put on the discussion table. To her, he was just a commoner in these lands, and he wanted to keep it that way for as long as he could. But regardless of those details, it was true that he had just happened to find her.

"I guess it was your lucky day," he teased. "Honestly, I was on my way to the forest when I saw someone. I watched for a minute, then I saw a pretty girl." She briefly wondered if that was a compliment or just a nicety to make her feel good. "When I saw you about to fall into the river, I ran. You know the rest." It wasn't a complete lie. He cut his eyes over to her. "I guess I'm your hero, now."

"Definitely right place, right time." Ellery made a face at his playful grandiosity.

He looked at her questioningly.

"It's a figure of speech. That I was lucky that you happened to come along at the same time that I… arrived." She figured that was the safest way to explain it. Not that she had any other way, she still had no idea what actually happened.

He nodded. "Or you could look at it from the perspective that I was supposed to be there." He paused for a minute and seemed to ponder the thought. "Maybe I was meant to find you."

She nodded slightly. "It's possible, I guess," she said with a nervous laugh. She wasn't ruling anything out at that point. "But that would make it…"

"Fate," he said flatly.

She went to laugh again but stifled it when she saw from the look on his face that he was serious. She mulled it over for a moment and though he was romanticizing the situation a bit. She couldn't blame him with what had just happened. Furthermore, if it was, in fact, fate, what did that mean? Why him? Why her for that matter, which was probably the biggest question to answer.

"I imagine not everyone would have an open mind like you to our situation," she said the last word with emphasis.

He knew that to be true but didn't want her to know just how true it was, or why. He had some suspicions about her and why she was there that he needed to think more about later. For now, he kept it light. "Maybe I am the lucky one," he said and sent her a quick grin.

Handsome and charming, she thought. "I wouldn't bet on it."

He was probably going to regret ever laying eyes on her by the time it was all said and done. Silence fell between them as they were both deep in their own thoughts.

"Is there magic in your world?" he asked and cut the silence.

What an odd question, she thought, but under the circumstances she could understand where he was coming from.

"Not the kind that you are thinking of." Although if he saw a car driving by, her cell phone, airplanes, or the internet, she thought maybe he would think of that as a bit of magic. "What about here?"

"It's complicated," he admitted, not knowing where to start with that answer, especially given his thoughts regarding her potential connection to his world.

She lifted her arm and pointed back toward herself. Inferring that it probably wasn't as complicated as them explaining how and why she was there. "Isn't it always?"

"Perhaps." But still he hesitated.

She wanted to push, but figured she was already pressing her luck. Besides, there was obviously more to that question than she originally thought. She still questioned how easily he was accepting everything.

"Does this sort of thing happen often?"

He looked at her and gave her an amused grin. "You mean, do beautiful women often appear before me?"

She couldn't help but laugh and blush at the compliment.

"Sadly, no. You are my first."

She smiled at him. He wasn't just handsome and charming, but from what she could tell, he was kind. There were worse ways to pass the time and certainly worse people to spend time with.

"What brought you out this way? I know you said that you were taking a trip. Business or pleasure?"

"Pleasure, because I need a break from business."

She nodded, understanding the preference for some personal space. She felt the need to circle back in their conversation, not being able to let it go. "You have to admit, you are taking this a lot better than most. That is, you don't seem surprised that I seemingly appeared out of thin air."

He looked over at her and lifted his eyebrows. "I'm glad it seems that way because when I first saw you it gave me quite a jolt. I'm still not sure I believe it. I keep telling myself maybe this is just a dream, and I will wake up in the morning wishing you had been real."

The sweet comment kept the heat on her cheeks, but she stayed silent as he continued.

"Anybody who met you, saw you, heard you, would know that there was something more to all of this. I would be a fool if I didn't believe what was right in front of my eyes. Besides, despite the absurdity of it all, it is also nice to take my mind off of things. You caught me at a bit of an impasse," he said. He surprised her by sharing so much. "Not just here and now, but in life."

She appreciated the fact that he was opening up to her as she had to him, in her own way. He didn't have to since she was the one at his mercy, and she thought highly of him because of it. She thought of what he said about his impasse.

"Are you running to or from something?"

That was a heck of a question, he thought and considered his answer. Oddly enough it was something that he had been asking himself since he left. "I am currently considering the merits of both options, and the latter is winning out. What about you? Where are you in your life?"

"I thought I was in a good place right where I was, next thing I know, I am here, so far away." She had been relatively happy, content at the very least. Wasn't that the same thing?

He smiled and considered her for a moment. "The world is full of mysteries."

She considered something of her own. "I wish I knew what this all meant. How I got here? Why? It is frustrating not being in control over my life."

It was something she often felt growing up. As she got older, she felt the need for that control more and more to the point where she wanted to be so independent that she tended to separate herself from everyone else.

"Let's consider it this way. It is safe for us to say that you aren't from here, but someone or something brought you here. Agreed?" he asked.

She nodded. She wasn't sure where he was going with it but was willing to follow along.

"When you decided to come with me into this forest you started making your own choices despite what brought you here. You took your control back."

She thought about it a moment and realized he was right. She had taken control back. She smiled to herself and felt a glimmer of hope.

CHAPTER SIX

To anyone else, they may have had the appearance of a young couple taking a hike through the woods, sneaking glances, speaking casually, and genuinely enjoying their time together. The time passed by with them talking about not much of anything, but she found that she enjoyed it. This was interesting because she normally loathed small talk.

There was already a level of comfort there with him that she didn't have with just anyone, and at one point when they walked in comfortable silence, she felt herself relax even further. She glanced over at him and not for the first time thought he was incredibly attractive. Her dreams did him no justice. Who he was right there in front of her was more than even her imagination could muster. She had the fleeting thought that he looked like a fairytale prince.

As if he sensed her stare he looked over. She had never seen eyes like his before. Gray but with flecks of what looked like gold. She couldn't help but let her gaze linger. She had been so caught up in her thoughts that she didn't see where she was walking and tripped on the uneven ground. He put an arm out to steady her and looked down at her boots.

"We will see what we can do about those later." Then he just had to ask, "What exactly are you wearing by the way?"

She had walked in front of him earlier, and he was concerned he was going to drool when he noticed that her jacket was cropped at her waist and showed the curve of her jeans from the back. He had too much going on in his mind when they met to think to ask, but now after some time, and a lot of additional study, he had to ask. He certainly wasn't going to let her walk around in that much longer. Once they were at the cottage, he would find something else for her to wear.

She took note that when he asked, his eyes quickly glanced down at her jeans. "You mean my clothes?"

"Yes," he said and tried to look away from the clothes in question, feeling it was safer to look at her face or straight ahead.

She looked at him, slightly affronted. "At home, my clothes are standard, stylish even." But she had a feeling that here, they would stick out like a sore thumb. Another piece of knowledge garnered that she tucked away.

"Your outfit is nice," he said, and she sensed a but coming, "but we are going to have to get you some clothes that will help you blend in here." Smoothly, he changed the topic away from a potential disagreement. "Are you hungry? We could stop for a snack."

She would have thought because of her nerves she would never want to eat again, but she realized that she was starving and nodded. He gestured to a fallen tree. She sighed with relief. She hadn't realized how tired she was until she sat. They had been going for a few hours.

Pure adrenaline carried her the first stretch of it. She went to reach for her cell phone now that they had a break, which was her usual way of things. Wanting to check the time and the weather, her email, random things she took for granted. It was somehow oddly relaxing and completely petrifying at the same moment without it.

"How close are we?" Not that it mattered. She would walk all night if she had to.

"Probably about an hour away yet." He stretched his own legs out before crossing them at the ankle. "In the past I often came here on horseback. This is certainly taking longer, but it's ranking as one of my favorite trips." He handed her an apple and put what looked to her like a leather canteen in between them.

She smiled. "Since this is the only trip I have taken in a very long time, I don't have much to rank it by."

"You don't take time for yourself much?" he asked before he bit into his own apple.

She shook her head. "Although, it is by choice," she admitted. She had the vacation time and the means to go if she really wanted to. But where would she go, and with whom? "I keep telling myself that one day I will take more time off, go on trips, even just to get out of the city on occasion."

"City?" He repeated the word. "What is a city, and why are you trying to get away from it?"

"It is a place. Where I live. We have more populated areas that we call cities, and less populated urban or rural areas." She briefly explained the difference between them, knowing if she got into too much detail they would be there all day. The stark differences between the two worlds could no doubt keep them entertained for a very long time.

"What is your housing like here, one-family dwellings for the most part?" From what she could glean from dreams that seemed to be the way of it. Besides the castle, of course.

He nodded in agreement. "More or less."

"I live in a building that holds many families."

"How many families does it hold?"

She thought of her apartment building. "It is a smaller one, probably only twenty or so."

He had to stop his jaw from physically dropping, but she didn't miss the look on his face.

"That is nothing. Some of the buildings are over a thousand feet tall."

He looked at her, awestruck. "You are joking."

She had to bite the inside of her cheek to keep from laughing. "Not one bit."

"What are they made out of?" The practical part of his mind was already taking over, thinking of the possibility of the construction.

"Many different things. It depends on the building and its use. Many of the largest buildings are made of steel."

He thought of his sword and tried to imagine buildings that seemed tall enough to touch the sky were made from the same steel of a sword as opposed to bricks or stone. After thinking on it for a minute, he had to admit that made sense. But another thing gave him pause. "How could you ever get to the top? Who could possibly climb that?"

She explained elevators.

He nodded absently, deep in thought.

"Doesn't that take a long time still?"

"They are pretty fast."

He went to ask how, and why, but he was already thinking of something else. He had a thousand questions swirling around in his mind as it went on overdrive. "Tell me something else that seems different."

She thought. "How do you communicate here? Sending letters?"

"Yes, pigeons, or horseback," he said matter-of-factly. "The pigeons are more efficient, so you don't always have to physically deliver the letter."

She explained texting and email, and he looked at her like she was a circus act. The explanation of technology clearly had him reeling.

"How do you travel?" he asked.

She was going to change the subject, but his excitement was infectious and his fascination clear. She looked at him, eyes sparkling, thinking how much he would enjoy riding in a fast car.

"How do you?" she answered his question with a question.

"Horse, or a horse and carriage."

She nodded. "Imagine the carriage without the horse, and one that can go much, much faster." She paused for effect. "Some even fly."

"How fascinating," he muttered to himself, as if trying to work it all out in his head. "What else?" He looked at her imploringly, and she smiled to herself, trying to imagine what he would do with Google.

"A lot," she said with emphasis. She tried to ask more about where he was from, but he seemed too enraptured with her world. She didn't realize at the time that he was putting her off from asking deeper questions of her own.

"What do you do for entertainment?"

At that she looked at him, smiled and told him of television, electronic tablets, and game consoles.

He shook his head in utter disbelief. "Remarkable."

She laughed as they hoisted up their packs and started back on their trek. He was in stunned silence. She could practically see the smoke coming out of his ears from the gears in his head spinning.

She tried to gauge the time of day. She had no idea what time it was but could tell by the position of the sun and the slight nip in the air that it was sometime in the evening. The sky began to turn an orange hue as if heralding the end of another day. Before long, darkness would descend, and she knew she didn't want to be in the middle of the forest when it came.

A part of her was relieved that they were going to head to a warm, cozy cabin and pack it in for the night, then start fresh. Maybe she wasn't ready for all the answers. Maybe she couldn't handle them. The whole thing seemed bigger than her. For the time being she was going to do the one thing she rarely ever did voluntarily, go with the flow.

They followed the light that was left of day still sifting through the trees. She thought of the forest, full of its shadows and mysteries, still not understanding that the most mysterious part of them was her.

~　~　~

The last stretch of their journey that should have been the longest seemed to fly by. She could tell they were getting closer because he seemed to tense up. He stilled for a minute, and she could see through the trees that there was a little clearing in the woods ahead. When they got to the edge of the forest there was a small cottage at the back of the clearing.

Her first thought was that the cottage looked like something from a painting. One she could see in a museum and wonder who was lucky enough to live there in that perfect little pocket in the glade. It would be a place for watching thunderstorms on the porch and sitting by the fire in the winter, a place to make memories with family.

Family.

She shoved that train of thought aside. Instead, she focused on finding out if there was a corner of that lovely cabin she could pass out in for the night and deal with the rest tomorrow. She trudged up the porch steps, the blisters that had formed on the back of her heels scraped with every step. She had to force herself not to cringe. She wanted to get the boots off and then find a place to collapse and something to curb the hunger in her stomach. She wanted to ask him if any of those were a possibility in the near future, but before she could say anything she saw the look on his face. It was somehow soft and intense at the same time. As if he was thinking of a sweet memory that was also incredibly painful and left a line of tension between his eyes. She wanted to lift her hand and smooth it with the pad of her thumb.

"Ready?" he asked and tried his best to smile at her, but the smile didn't reach his eyes.

She nodded and followed him. "When did you say was the last time that you were here?"

"Many years ago," he answered absently, his mind elsewhere.

"And this is a friend's cottage?" she pressed but he simply nodded as he pushed the door open and walked inside.

She followed and took in the cabin's comforting atmosphere as she removed her shoes. The last of the evening light filtered through the windows. It gave everything a cozy glow. She looked at Alexei whose features were now masked by a neutral facade. For a moment she wondered if she had imagined that pained look on his face, but she knew she hadn't. Were the memories still so vivid despite the years that had passed and what had they dredged up inside of him? Despite his indifference, she could tell that something lingered, and as he moved forward, she decided to give him space to sort it out.

She took in her surroundings. The living room was the first to greet her. When she took a step, she felt a soft blue rug against her feet that covered much of the wood floor and added a touch of color to the otherwise muted decor. The room was furnished in a way that made it feel warm and inviting. Wanting to give him space she sat at the end of a well-worn sofa that was positioned in front of a fireplace.

Chapter Seven

After making a fire in the hearth in the front room, Alexei went to the kitchen and laid out grapes, almonds, cheese, dried meat, and slices of bread, then boiled water on the stove for tea. It wasn't anything fancy, more like a tray of snacks, but it would do. His stomach tightened as he walked back into the room. He was half afraid that when he walked back in that she would be gone, like she had never been there. Despite all rational thinking, that left an empty feeling inside him.

The knot in his stomach loosened when he saw her curled on the end of a couch under a blanket. Relief, along with a feeling of protectiveness, flooded through him at the sight of her. He hadn't often been in a position growing up where he needed to take care of someone. Instead, someone often filled that role for him, but he found that he liked the feeling of being a protector. It struck him that he would need that in his line of work, so it was a good thing that it was sitting well with him. She opened her eyes and smiled at him as shadows from the fire danced on the walls behind her. Her smile spread wider when she saw what he had in his hands. He placed the tray on the table in front of her.

"Oh," she exclaimed. "It looks like a charcuterie board."

"What is that?" he asked as he looked down at the food with a questioning stare.

She laughed again. "It is just a nice way to present food."

He watched as she took a grape and popped it into her mouth. Her eyes closed when the sweetness and the smallest hint of tang hit. She opened them and saw that he was staring at her fixedly. She blushed. Had anyone ever looked at her like that before, so thoroughly?

"Thank you. This is perfect," she said.

He enjoyed having her there and sharing a meal with her. Although that was a loose term for the food that they were eating, it was still nice just the same. They ate in silence for a few minutes. She watched as he headed back to the kitchen and came back with two steaming mugs in his hands. He sat back on the other end of the couch, and she spread out the blanket and offered him half.

He passed a mug to her. "Tea, with brandy in it," he said in explanation. "It'll help to soothe the rough edges."

She held the mug and took a tentative sip. Although she wouldn't be trading in her iced lattes anytime soon, she had to admit it wasn't bad. The combination of the warm tea and brandy was comforting. She sipped slowly and felt her anxiety fade as warmth spread throughout her body. Soon the tension inside softened its hold, and she leaned back into the cushions.

She knew she shouldn't pry but couldn't help but ask. "Why are you really here?"

He studied her before answering, as if making a decision. "My parents passed away years ago, and my uncle has raised me since. He had taken over the family business until I was old enough. It was time for me to take over the family business, so I left."

"Do you not like the job?"

There was no way for her to know how heavy and important the answer was, or how complicated. "It's not that I don't like it. I worry I won't be any good at it. It isn't exactly something that I can fail at."

"That is going to be a problem then because failing is inevitable. We all fail sometimes. The people you work with will be more concerned with how you handle those failures."

He smiled to himself. He had never thought of it like that before. He thought of his parents and his uncle, they always seemed so perfect, so put together, but he knew he was as human as everyone else. That thought gave him hope. "That is a good way to look at it."

For a time after the only noise was the fire crackling as they finished their tea, each lost in their own thoughts. In the quiet, a thought crossed her mind. "What did you mean earlier when you asked me about magic?"

She was surprised when he answered. "They say this world was once filled with wonder and magic." He moved to add a log to the fire. He gave her a minute to take in the information before he sat back down and looked to her for her thoughts.

She looked at him in disbelief but asked, "There is no magic now?"

He shook his head. "As far as I know, the only magic left is what is talked about in stories."

Ellery couldn't believe what she was hearing. She had read about magic in books but never thought it could be real. If he was right, it had existed in these lands at one point. "That's impossible," she breathed.

He should have left it at that, but he didn't. "I bet this morning you also didn't believe in any world beyond your own."

"Touché," she said.

She wondered if magic truly existed beyond someone's imagination, beyond the words on a page. Enchanting stories of magic and fantasy worlds filled bookshelves all over the world. Could there be even a kernel piece of truth within any of them? Then she thought of her own dreams and looked at the living, breathing, beautiful proof in front of her. How had she been so quick to dismiss it?

He saw she was still deep in thought and tired, which was good. He wanted to distract her. They had gone far enough for one night. "Anyway," he lifted his hands and wiggled his fingers. "No magic here if that is what you are wondering."

She was tired, but her mind was still reeling. Is that how she got here? It couldn't be. She didn't realize she said it out loud when she saw him shrug his shoulders.

The harder she tried to think, the quicker she started to doze, and he was grateful for it. It would give him time to think of how to handle the situation in the morning. He didn't want to admit anything further, for both of their sakes and was relieved when her eyes finally closed. He let out a sigh.

He would tell her everything he knew, but not yet. He stood to get something for her to wear for bed. He entered one of the bedrooms and pulled out a nightgown, smoothing a hand against it and trying to push away the memories that were threatening to flood through. He scanned the room and decided she could stay there, and he would take the room across the hall.

He returned to the living room with old memories haunting him every step of the way. The only thing that quieted them was when he stared at her, because then everything else in his head seemed to disappear.

She looked so peaceful when he leaned down and gently brushed aside a strand of hair from her face before gently shaking her shoulder, hoping to waken her without startling her. Her eyes slowly opened, and she looked up at him with a confused expression. He offered her a gentle smile and saw the exact moment when recognition flickered across her face, and she offered him a sleepy smile.

"I'm sorry, I must've dozed off."

"You had a long day, to say the least. Let's get you to bed," he said softly and reached out a hand. "I laid something out for you in one of the bedrooms."

He walked her back to the bedroom and leaned against the doorframe as she walked to the bed and ran her hand down the nightgown he had laid out. She turned back to meet his eyes. "Maybe this really is all just a dream, and I'll wake up in the morning at home."

The thought was like a punch in his gut. He forced himself to smile at her reassuringly. "If so, it was nice meeting you."

He turned to leave and looked back over his shoulder at her meaningfully. Her long, brown hair fell loosely around her and her hazel eyes stared back at him. He couldn't imagine what she was going through, but instead of crumbling under the weight of it all, she held her head high. He felt a pull toward her so strong that because of that, he tore his gaze away. Despite the fact that he was tempted to do otherwise. "Come visit me in dreams anytime." He offered her a smile.

He closed the door tightly behind him and stood for a minute leaning against it. He knew he wouldn't be any good to her if he was exhausted, so he went into the other bedroom and got ready for bed. His mind raced with the thoughts he had kept from her. Stories that he had been told over the years of magic and those who wielded it… and those who vanquished it.

Then, his thoughts turned to her, of who she might be and what part in those stories she might play. He had no idea what brought her there, magic or fate, both, but he knew he wasn't ready to let her go. He stripped down and slid between the cool sheets, thinking he would sleep and see what tomorrow brought. That night when he dreamt, he dreamt of magic, of it being restored, of it being vanquished for good, and at every turn, she was there.

~   ~   ~

Ellery couldn't remember the last time she slept so well. She woke up in stages. So warm and content, not quite ready to open her eyes. It wasn't often she lounged in bed and told herself just a little bit longer. Though when she moved her arm to bring the blanket up around her neck, she felt the soft, long sleeve of the nightgown against her skin.

"I'm still here!" she cried out softly. Her heart leapt within her. "Is this good or bad? Shouldn't I be waking up from this dream in my own bed?"

The day before flooded her mind like scenes from a movie. The incredible feelings of waking up there, the first moment she saw Alexei, ending the day with him in this sweet cottage that felt like a home. It was still so surreal and even though she had no idea what was going to happen next, she wasn't going to miss a second of it. She rolled out of bed and put her clothes from the previous day back on.

She walked out past the bedroom and back to the main living area. She saw the empty wooden tray Alexei had brought out the night before. The thought of it, and him, brought a smile to her face. Ellery opened the door and stepped outside. She felt trapped. She needed to figure out why she was caught in the realm of her dreams. A realm that was somehow real. She tried not to make too much noise as she shut the door behind her. He needed to sleep. While she enjoyed his company immensely, she still relished the quiet.

She took her time as she walked the edge of the small clearing as the sun rose and the dew felt cool and wet beneath her feet.

"Everything feels real." She couldn't understand it. She should be waking up in her apartment right now.

"What is happening?" she whispered to the open air around her.

The air smelled of pine and wildflowers. It was intoxicating. He was intoxicating. Who would have thought that she would have met the handsome stranger who had stepped out of her dreams and into her life.

Her steps slowed, and she stopped to pick a daisy that grew wild amongst the tall grasses. She crouched down, gently plucking it from where it grew. When she lifted her head, she slowly let the flower slip through her fingers.

I shouldn't have strayed from the cabin.

A man stepped into view, and she slowly backed up. Hairs on the back of her neck stood up as she took him in. When their eyes met, chills of fear ran through her. His smooth movements caused his raven black hair to sway as it brushed against the nape of his neck, as if blown by a breeze. His movement was animalistic, instinctual, there was no question he knew exactly where he was going and what he wanted. It was the same self-assurance that sparked in his light blue eyes. A beautiful blue that stuck out even more against his black rimmed irises. The color was too piercing. She felt them penetrate her entire being with a glance, and it didn't take her long to note that there was something cold behind them as they studied every inch of her. He was communicating without words, and, while she didn't understand exactly what he was saying, she was sure it was something she didn't want to know.

She tore her focus from his eyes and looked him over once more as his mouth cocked up into a smirk. His features were prominent, and his face was all strong lines and sharp angles, as though he had been personally crafted by an overly-aggressive sculptor – it was a look that worked wonders for him. The black shirt, vest, and trousers that he wore were similar to Alexei's. They didn't do anything to disguise the powerful build of his body underneath. She didn't see any softness anywhere on him and under other circumstances might have enjoyed taking in the virile man that was slowly invading her space.

But not today. Not here, when she was alone.

He was handsome, but her instincts told her his inside didn't quite match up with the beauty of the outside. A few other men came out behind him on either side, although she didn't get a good look at them. They seemed like a blur, as her eyes were solely fixed on the man in front of her, worrying that if she took her eyes off of him it would be her last mistake.

"Good morning." His voice seemed to fill the clearing with a quiet intensity that made her stomach clutch. When his gaze landed on her clothes, interest sparked in his eyes. "Aren't you just as pretty as the sunshine this morning."

CHAPTER EIGHT

Cold sweat dripped down Ellery's back. She was looking trouble right in the face and had no idea how to save herself. She instinctively stepped back, her heart beating fast. He kept advancing with predatory steps, each move toward her deliberate and slow. She bumped up against something or someone. It made her jump in surprise. Alarm bells went off in her mind when she felt someone's hands grabbing onto her upper arms.

She jerked her arms free and looked around.

Crap.

There were more with him than she thought. At every angle another man stood. She counted six in all. Each wore a vest that had the same emblem on it, a wolf that stood tall and proud. Her thoughts were interrupted as he crooned behind her, and she turned around to meet his gaze.

"Are you alone?" His voice was velvety and seemed to ooze out of him. He had the upper hand, and he knew it.

"I don't need a babysitter," she said in answer, leaving Alexei out of it.

"You don't want to be alone in these woods. Who knows what kind of trouble you might find yourself in."

"I can handle myself."

As calmly as she could she went to move past him and he stepped in her way, resting his hand on the hilt of a long blade sheathed at his hip. She wondered if he would use that blade on her. She saw the flash of something in his eyes that told her he would be more than happy to.

"It wasn't a question." His smile turned into a sneer, and she wanted to wipe it off his mouth.

"Condescending prick," she muttered.

"What was that, sweetheart?"

"I said if you are so worried about who is roaming these woods, why aren't you out wandering around? As I said, I can handle myself." She appeared as nonchalant as possible and went to walk by again.

Before she could react, he grabbed her by the shoulders and pulled her closer to him. He leaned down to whisper into her neck like a lover. She felt his warm breath mix with the cool air against her skin, and she forced herself not to tense.

"Let's not make this any harder than it needs to be or you are going to quickly realize that I can be what you don't want to run into around here. It is up to you, we can either do this as easy, or as rough," he said with sickening emphasis squeezing her arms hard enough to make her want to wince, "as you want to."

Her fist clenched, and she wanted nothing more than to plant it in his face, but she knew better than to make a move now. He let her go, and she stepped back. She wasn't stronger than them, but there was a solid chance that she was smarter. She needed to distract… and then fool them.

On my left, the big guy with hairy arms… no weapons. Her eyes swiveled to the next would-be attacker. *Skinny guy, mean eyes. Strong arms.* She took inventory of them all and quickly planned it out in her head until she was ready. Time for Act One of her plan. She peered over his shoulder and plastered a look of confusion on her face. The whole gamut—wide eyes, trembling lips. Then, she let it fade into raw fear. She saw his face shift into his own look of confusion. To finish her performance, she let out a bloodcurdling scream.

He turned along with the others beside him, and although she couldn't see the ones behind her, she ran toward the one that didn't have a sword or dagger sheathed on his belt. Although he was quick, she was quicker and just escaped his arm when he saw that she was running past. It didn't take them long to realize what happened. She knew six grown men were on her tail. Too bad she didn't have a plan past Act One.

She should run to the cabin, but she didn't want Alexei to get involved. She tore off toward the direction that they came in the night before. There were two tall trees that they walked between the night before. She thought of what was just inside those woods and ways that she could lose the men. She didn't have the skill to climb up a tree fast enough before they got there to hide. She tried to think of any big rocks that she had seen that she could use for cover. Nothing came to the forefront of her mind that would give her a chance of effectively losing them.

Hell with it. She wouldn't last long trying to outrun them. Without any prospects of safety and not knowing the terrain, it was inevitable that they'd catch her. She could keep running and do her best or she could turn around and fight. Her legs were burning already. She turned around and faced them, raising her fists and preparing for the onslaught. No matter what happened, she wasn't going to make it pleasant for them.

Her heart pounded from the adrenaline. Was she going to be sick? Not exactly the best time to vomit her guts up. Whatever had been building was pushed back down when she caught a movement out of the corner of her eye. She looked over to see Alexei running toward her. Relief flooded through her at the sight of him, but at the same time she wanted to tell him to keep running and save himself.

When he reached her, she was taken aback by the way his gray eyes blazed, and when they latched onto her, the look left something unspoken between them. She experienced an unfamiliar thrill at the sight of him and feelings that she had no business feeling rushed up inside of her. Before he broke his gaze, he slightly shook his head "no," relaying to her to be quiet as he reached her and pulled her behind him. He spoke low enough so only she could hear.

"Whatever you hear, go along with it. I'll explain later."

Then he faced forward and spoke to the men who were seconds away. Ellery thought he was certifiably nuts to think six on one was good odds for him. He was surely going to get them both killed. Her mind was already trying to formulate a new plan with him being factored into it when she heard what came out next.

"Do you want to explain yourself, Aines?" Alexei barked out.

Wait, what? Alexei *knew* him. He called that man by name. She looked from behind his back as the men stopped abruptly. It would have been comedic the way they stopped like they had run into a brick wall if the situation hadn't been so awful. The man who had threatened her had his sneer replaced with recognition, confusion and then reluctantly, very reluctantly, fear.

"Forgive us, Your Highness. We didn't know that it was you." He sounded anything but sorry. Ellery saw the others kneel.

Anger laced with ice edged Alexei's voice. Although she hadn't known him long, she was shocked by his tone. "Is this how you treat the people in my kingdom? Especially unarmed women? You are soldiers. Your job is to protect people, not harm them."

My kingdom. Your Highness. She couldn't have heard that right, she thought hazily, trying to clear her mind of all the racing thoughts. She saw it then, the look about him, the tone of his voice, and the way that he carried himself. His presence was powerful and commanding. It seemed to fill the entire glade. Even his words carried a certain weight that demanded attention.

"No, Your Highness," a few of them said in unison with their heads bowed.

"That's good, or I would have to discharge you." He shook his head in obvious disgust. "Although, I just might when I get home, regardless. What are you doing here? This is a long way from your regular patrol."

Aines stood a little straighter at that question and gained some of his composure back. "First, we were sent to find you. Then, you can imagine our surprise when we came upon this delectable little wench instead." He glanced at Ellery, and slowly, deliberately raked his eyes over her clothing, and looked back at Alexei with a sardonic look. "I'm sure you are aware of what the king will think she…" He never got to finish his statement.

"I'm well aware," Alexei snapped, not letting the man continue. "I have it under control. She is with me."

"She said she was alone."

"Does she look like she is alone?" he demanded impatiently. "Go home. I will take it from here."

"Is this a command from our prince, or as her lover?"

"That's none of your damn business, Aines, but if you care that much, you can pick either option as long as you understand that she is with me."

Silence filled the glade at the implication of what he just said. He didn't care what they thought as long as they understood his message.

"Why don't you pack up, and we will escort you both back to the safety of the palace."

"That won't be necessary."

"I insist," Aines said with cold hatred in his eyes.

"Watch yourself," Alexei spat out with lethal calmness, not wanting to turn this into something they couldn't get back from.

"The king isn't going to be happy."

"Interim king," he corrected. "Bear in mind who will be your king soon. Your future in my army is at risk, soldier."

Anger still seethed through Aines, but fear for his status as a king's soldier won out. "My apologies," he said and bowed his head to hide the look of hatred in his eyes. Their dislike for each other was obvious.

"My uncle will have to be made aware of your actions here today. If you find any other unarmed, innocent bystanders on the way back to the castle, try not to accost them."

Aines bowed stiffly again and nodded to the others. As they began to walk back through the woods, Aines turned to give Ellery one last look that said he wasn't done with her yet. Alexei felt her tense behind him. A part of Alexei wanted to handle the situation then and there, make an example of the man, but he needed to take care of Ellery first. He clenched his fists and forced himself to stay where he was. Aines' time would come—he would make sure of it.

Alexei waited until they got out of earshot until they started talking, not wanting to give the men anything else to tell the king, but naturally she was off the mark and the green in her hazel eyes seemed brighter, like a sea witch's, as they threw daggers at him. "Do you want to explain what the hell just happened?

Alexei turned to face her, but she had placed her hands on her hips. He felt a rush of guilt, but he knew that the question was necessary. He had others to think about and protect. "I can explain," he said.

She snapped at him. "Explain what? Your lackey's callous behavior or your own lies to me."

"They will be dealt with, and I didn't lie. I may have withheld the full truth, but there is more than just me to consider."

"Who are you?"

"My name is Alexei, exactly what I told you."

"How can I be sure of anything? Of you? You obviously know them." She pointed toward the forest where the men had retreated and shot him an accusatory look.

For a moment, Alexei closed his eyes and tried to be calm. He'd had a restless night. He was tired, baffled by everything that had happened, and wasn't sure what to do next. The weight of the whole kingdom was on his shoulders and all he seemed to care about was the welfare and safety of the one person in front of him who looked like she would gladly murder him in her anger. Sadly, calm did not win out.

"Do you want me to ask the same of you? There are plenty of questions that I could ask for a straight answer to."

If he had expected her to shrink back into herself and pout over his outburst, he would have been sadly mistaken. Not only did she not shy away, she kept her eyes locked on his. No one dared look at him like that. Most people acted either fawning or fearful, even though he could have done without either. But not her, and goodness help him if it didn't make him want her more. He couldn't help but respect her defiance, even if it wasn't something he was used to.

"Please tell me that this is all some mix-up."

He wondered what happened to her in the past that even in the midst of a complete upheaval she was able to keep everything in check. It was like she was able to read minds because her eyes narrowed.

"I don't need your pity." There was an edge in that statement that was sharp.

"I didn't say I pitied you. I certainly haven't treated you like I have."

"You didn't have to. I could see it in your haughty eyes."

He threw his hands in the air in frustration before running them through his hair. "What do you want from me, Ellery? Of course I feel bad for you. I'm human."

"That's it. I'm done." She turned in the opposite direction and began stalking away.

He called after her, "You can't do this alone."

She turned to look back at him and anger flashed in her eyes bright and hot. He kept talking anyway.

"You may think you can, but we both know that you can't, and you aren't reckless."

So odd that she knew him, had seen him, wrote of him, wanted him. It was as if she had willed herself to him. Is that why she felt betrayed? She knew that she had no real reason to feel this way. He didn't know her, not the way that she knew him. Not the way that she thought she had known him. He had been the one thing that felt real in that world of fantasy and dreams.

Despite all of it, she knew deep down that she could trust him and guilt filtered through the anger. She just wished he would have appeared in her dreams lazing on a throne with a glittering gold crown on his head instead of the dozens of other ways she saw him. She was completely blindsided. Since she still held that part of her back, the dreams, she couldn't explain the extent of her emotions. He probably thought she had completely lost it. Still, she had to know how he felt, so she stopped and turned around.

"Was this some type of game, your last little adventure before you become… become …" She threw her hands in the air and twirled them in circles symbolizing a crown. "King?"

She thought of his talk of fate, and the way he had looked after her. She remembered the first time he saw her, and the intrigue, not the shock.

"Was there not enough going on at the palace for you so you had to get out to find something diverting, and oh boy, how lucky for you when you stumbled across poor little old me. How happy for you that you found me to be your distraction."

"It's not like that," he bit out and walked toward her.

"Just don't." She reached out a hand to his chest to stop him from coming closer, and he moved to cover it with his own until he saw the way that she instantly paled. Pure shock was across her face. He followed her gaze and felt his own shock reverberate through his body.

"That's just not possible," she stammered and jumped back.

She cautiously flexed her too-warm hands as light coming from her fingertips felt like raw energy, sending tingles down her spine. She'd felt this before, back home, just never this strong.

She couldn't quite understand how this was real as she watched as the light danced along her skin. Is that what she had been feeling the last couple of days? Was it this, just waiting to be released? As she stood there, her hands aglow with untapped power, she couldn't help but feel both exhilarated and terrified. The concept seemed absurd, laughable. Yet, here she was, standing in a world where magic not only existed, but it was coursing through her body and answering to something inside of her.

"The light coming out of your fingers would say otherwise."

She raised her hands between them and stared at them like she had never seen them before.

"Who are you?" he asked although it seemed rhetorical.

There was a quiet intensity in his gaze. He looked at her as if she couldn't possibly be real, like he was seeing things. He outstretched a hand, pausing midair and searching her eyes for approval. She nodded and his hands gently touched one of her own. He lifted it so he could look, turning it over, then trailing strong fingers down her arm. The touch seemed to tingle wherever his finger trailed, leaving a shock to her system.

She didn't understand how such an innocent touch seemed to leave an invisible mark on her skin. He didn't linger, except for with his eyes, as he pulled his hand back.

She wondered if he felt the same sudden shock from the touch as she did, because as he lifted his hand away from her skin he glanced down briefly with an odd look on his face.

"Looks like we have even more to talk about on our travels than I thought. I know we have about a million things to talk about, but none of it is anything that we can solve in the next five minutes. Let's go back to the cottage and pack up. We will have the whole day to deal with the rest."

He was right, she had wanted to press for answers, but also knew that they would have plenty of time to talk that day. When he turned back toward the cottage, he reached out a hand for hers, and she took it.

"What now, Your Highness. Do I curtsy?" she teased and tried to lighten the mood.

"I'm the same person I was an hour ago."

The way he looked at her she could tell he meant it. She nodded but knew in his world he would never just be Alexei and decided to change the subject entirely. "I'm assuming this isn't a friend's cottage?"

"It is my family's," he confirmed. Something in his tone made her think that it wasn't up for discussion, so she followed his lead and moved on.

"What's next after we head out?"

"You'll see."

"I'll see," she muttered.

The look on his face said that he wanted to roll his eyes heavenward, but to his credit he didn't, even though hers were shooting daggers at him. "Would you believe me if I said the lack of details is for your safety?"

"What aren't you telling me? What are you really worried about?"

"Your safety," he repeated.

"Why safety?" she said warily. She was sick of him talking in circles.

"Let's not talk about this right now. I don't even know if any of my suspicions are right."

He would need to tell her sooner rather than later about the link she might have there in Westrim. If anyone thought of that, coupled with the fact that she essentially fell out of the sky, he would never get her to safety. He was lucky he had been able to keep her safe that morning. He knew what Aines was referring to when he mentioned what Carwyn had assumed, and how it all could have ended a lot differently.

"I can't say I will tell you my suspicions right away, but I can promise you there won't be any more secrets between us from here on out."

"Okay," she said, not wanting to fight with a man she already had so many conflicting feelings about.

Even though the biggest part of her wanted to dig in and get the answers out of him, she held her tongue. Instead, she decided to take a leap of faith. She wasn't an overly trusting person and essentially never let things go. She was a dog with a bone until she had a situation figured out after overanalyzing it to death. Everything about this whole experience was new to her.

"I want to pack some things up before we go and also get you changed. I have some stuff for you to wear and extras to bring along." He could still see the way Aines' eyes roamed over her body. He wanted to knock the man's eyes right out of his head.

"I know I'm not exactly inconspicuous, but I think we have a bigger problem. I'll be traveling with a crowned prince who is playing hooky, and you are worried about someone spotting me."

Not that she wasn't right, but she would certainly capture a lot more attention than she realized. A t-shirt and breeches weren't truly going to camouflage her, everything about her seemed to radiate that she was different.

"Nothing we can do about that now. Let's go get you those clothes and get moving."

CHAPTER NINE

After they left the cottage, she told him what happened that morning before he jumped in and how thankful she was for it. She couldn't imagine the walk she would be having through the woods with that group right now if Alexei hadn't come along. Something told her it wouldn't have ended well for her.

"So, if you are the prince in this story, what does that make me, the damsel?" she asked, raising a skeptical brow.

"Far from it," he said and laughed ruefully. "A fight of six to one wasn't fair to start with, and not many of my own soldiers could have gotten out of a situation like that."

"Looks like you need a new training regimen," she teased. "Seriously though, it wasn't like I took them all down in hand-to-hand combat. I outwitted them, and that isn't the same."

"Give yourself more credit. You did well."

"Thanks." Her cheeks heated at the compliment. "So, were you ever planning on telling me that you were a prince?"

He nodded his head and leveled a look at her. "Sure, in the same conversation when you told me that you were magic."

"I'm not," she protested. What the hell was she? "I can't be. Magic doesn't even exist outside of fiction."

"In your world neither do I, but here I am."

She tried to reason with her hormones to get their act together and concentrate but she thought of him in her world and wondered if she could take him back with her as a souvenir.

"What brought you here if not magic?" he asked and cut into her thoughts of how expensive it would be to send him home by overnight mail.

"If I was magic, wouldn't I know? I'm twenty-one years old. How would I have gone my whole life without knowing?"

"Maybe your powers are somehow tied to proximity?"

She blew out her breath and considered his words. Then as it normally did, her mind started to go a million miles an hour. He must have seen that she was working something out in her head because he stayed silent and waited.

"For argument's sake let's say I'm buying into all this. If we follow your train of thought, maybe I had to be here for it to fully manifest. To be somewhere where there are other sources of magic for it to spark."

"Maybe it is waking up a bit. Like it doesn't have a foothold yet and needs to gain some traction," Alexei offered.

"You really believe this don't you? I mean, how are you even sure that it is magic?"

"Is it normal in your world for people to have light shooting out of their fingertips?"

"Not exactly," she said sheepishly.

She thought of magic in her world. In the realm of popular fiction magical powers usually came with robes and wands, not whatever misfit powers she was somehow displaying.

"What would your first instinct be if you did see that happening to someone?" he asked.

"Most likely that I had gone completely and utterly mad."

He laughed. "I don't think you are mad." He reached out and brushed the back of his knuckles across her cheek. "I think you are magic."

Maybe it was magic that had her feeling like she had goosebumps roving her body and not his touch.

"There is only one way to prove it. Why don't you try it again?" he encouraged her.

"I'm not even sure how I did it the first time."

"Just try."

She shrugged. What could it hurt?

Then, she cleared her throat and moved to crack her neck before sticking her hands out, palms up. She lifted them up and down. Then she held them straight up and down and pushed out like she could force it. When that didn't work, she cupped them together in front of her and waited a few seconds before opening them slowly, as if there would be some magical energy hovering there.

Then, he could see her wheels turning as she used her one finger like a wand and swished it in the air. After a while they started walking again as she kept trying. At one point she flicked her wrist, and he swore she muttered the word web. He wasn't even going to ask about that one.

After a while he stopped and turned toward her. She followed suit.

"Try to concentrate," he said.

She leveled a stare at him. "What exactly do you think I've been doing?"

"I think that brilliant mind of yours is running full steam and can't concentrate on any one thing. Try to clear it."

She wanted to tell him that was impossible, that no amount of meditation and yoga had ever been enough to quiet it down. Instead, she nodded and closed her eyes, but she felt ridiculous and held back a laugh.

"Concentrate." He lowered his voice and rested his hands on her shoulders for support. "Relax and clear your mind. Close your eyes and focus on what you want."

She was sure she was supposed to be thinking of the white lights coming from her like she was some avenging angel, but instead all she saw was him. She pictured him looking down at her and thought of those hands roaming over the rest of her body, not chastely holding onto her shoulders. Then that tingling, that warmth and energy, built up inside of her, although that feeling had to be from desire not magic.

She heard his intake of breath. She opened her eyes to see a small ball of light cupped in her hands, and before she could try anything it started to flicker and sputter out like a dying lightbulb.

"What happened?" He pulled back, his eyes still glued to her hands.

"I think I broke my concentration. I'll try again."

She tried and epically failed again and again. She focused on the feeling of that warm energy that she had felt pulsing through her hands, the gentle wave of power that had radiated from her palms. She imagined shaping it, controlling it. But no matter how hard she tried, nothing seemed to work. Frustrated and exhausted, she decided to take a break as she felt her head start to throb.

She let out a frustrated sigh. "I feel like I'm missing something, but I don't know what." When he didn't say anything, she looked over at him and he seemed to be mulling something over.

"Everything okay?"

He nodded but there was a crease between his brows still. "I feel like I missed something too. I've been turning something over in my head that you said earlier."

"What?"

"You said maybe you had to be here for your magic to *fully* manifest. Meaning that some part of you had wielded it before?"

She tried not to cringe at her slip-up. "Not exactly. It's complicated."

"I think I can keep up," he said a bit dryly.

"I never wielded magic. I had some feeling building up inside of me, but it never turned into what it did today."

"So, you had felt it before?"

She nodded. "It started happening the day before I woke up here."

"You didn't think that was worth mentioning?"

"There is more to it, and I wasn't sure how much I could trust you, or anyone, with it."

"I think we are past that now."

That was true, and because it was, she decided to tell him. "I was writing of this place before I woke up here." She looked away, afraid of what she might see on his face. She had given him such a hard time earlier about honesty, all the while knowing she was holding back. Out of the corner of her eye she saw him pin her with a stare.

"Go on. You can't stop there." But the eyes that had been locked on hers looked away when she met them.

After everything that he had done for her and continued to do, she owed him at least that much. "A few months ago, on my twenty-first birthday I started having what you could call unconventional dreams." She stopped, realizing how it sounded, but there was no turning back now. "I often dreamt before, but this felt different somehow."

"What did you see in these dreams?" His face, his voice, was neutral. She told him of her dreams with as much detail as possible. The beauty of them, the energy within them, and the awareness.

"I could feel the sun on my face and the breeze in my hair. I could feel a horse underneath me as it galloped, and a dress swish around my legs as I danced. It was like I was somehow connected to them." It sounded absurd but she didn't know how else to explain it. It had felt like there was a link between herself and the world that she had found herself in. She paused as silence sat between them. "Sometimes you were there," she added quietly and saw his body tense.

"I could see you, but you couldn't see me. No one could. It was like I was an invisible spectator to the daily lives of others. And you," she said and motioned to him. "You were as you are now. You didn't look like a prince. It certainly would have been easier to see you in a throne room as opposed to riding horses, writing, or working out." He had often been training, which made sense as he was also a soldier, and the writing was directly tied to the politics of it all. She assumed there was a lot of that when you were a royal. "I guess I assumed that, well I don't know what I thought, actually."

"Are you so quick to write off fate now?" he asked, and she shook her head. "Where we are heading is the only place that might have that kind of power to pull you through your reality into mine."

"Where does that leave us?" She expected him to be mad and wasn't quite ready to meet his eyes. He moved to her and put two of his fingers gently under her chin and turned her face to him.

He looked at her meaningfully. "We are fine."

"I'm sorry that I didn't tell you."

He shrugged. "I'm sure there is a lot more that we will uncover about each other." He still couldn't bring himself to tell her that last secret that he was keeping—who and what he thought she may be. Instead, he moved his hand but then put it back at his side. He tried not to think of how badly he wanted to touch her. It wasn't the time or the place for what he wanted, and kissing her senseless certainly wasn't what she needed.

She touched him in a way that no one had before. He wanted, needed to be there for her. It was a need that took root inside of him, despite the many reasons not to get attached. Something in her called to him, and he tried to remind himself of all the reasons to ignore it.

She looked serious and strained, and he didn't like seeing her like that. He decided to lighten the mood. "So, I'm the man of your dreams?" He sent her a cocky grin when her head shot over, and her eyes locked with his. "What was I wearing in these dreams?"

He gave a self-satisfied smile when he saw her cheeks heat. She opened and closed her mouth twice before she gave up and laughed.

They'd made good progress on their journey, and he hadn't noticed how late it had gotten. But as the sun faded away, it was time to stop for the night.

He turned to tell Ellery and saw her squinting at the light that fought its way through the trees. She looked like she was in pain.

Ellery began to panic when she felt all the tells of a migraine coming on. The most brutal ones came swiftly, and that was exactly what happened. The pain was sudden and relentless. It was like all the building tension that she had kept at bay since she got there was let loose. It felt like an invisible vise had clamped down on her head, and it squeezed tighter with every passing second. Her vision blurred from the building pressure at her temples.

"Why don't we stop for the night? It is starting to get dark." he said, sounding a bit too nonchalant.

Ellery knew he was doing it for her benefit. He looked calm but concerned. Despite the fact that she had started seeing spots in her eyes, her stubbornness clamored and told her to keep going so she shook her head. "We still have some daylight. Let's keep going."

The thought of being the weak link pushed her onward, but each minute the pressure and pain worsened, and a sheen of sweat built on her face.

He swore she got paler by the minute, and he couldn't take it anymore. He reached out and laid a hand on her arm, stopping them both. When she looked at him, he felt awful he hadn't stopped her sooner. She swayed on her feet, and he solved the problem by scooping her up and holding her high against his chest. She closed her eyes against a wave of nausea and figured it would be even worse if she threw up on him, so she kept her eyes closed. When she felt him walking down a hill, she opened them long enough to watch as he walked down the side of an embankment and sat with his back against a tree at the bottom as he settled her in his lap.

She was desperate for relief from the pain and let out a low moan when she felt the arm around her rub at her temples, then move down to her neck, kneading. He murmured to her. Through the haze of pain, she wasn't exactly sure what he said, but it was comforting. She realized that this would have been a nice moment under different circumstances. Sitting in his lap while he held her close, he leaned down and gently whispered for her to go to sleep. With the intense pressure still building, she couldn't do anything else and closed her eyes.

When he was sure she was asleep he still cradled her against him with one arm and with the other he positioned one of the packs beside him as a pillow before he gently eased her away from him and laid her down, careful not to wake her. He reached for the second pack and pulled out a blanket to cover her. He watched over her as she slept.

He had to continuously stop himself from reaching out and touching her, but he knew that she needed the rest. After a while he decided to head back up the embankment and look around. He didn't think there was anything to worry about, but he also figured a bit of space would do him good.

CHAPTER TEN

Ellery was relieved hours later when she opened her eyes that the incessant pressure was gone. There was still a dull throb, but the worst of it had passed. The first thing that caught her attention was the makeshift bed Alexei had made. She was using one of the packs as a pillow and had been tucked in with a blanket.

The second thing she noticed when she woke up was that he had gone. She sat up frantically, looking for any trace of him among the trees, but all she could see were his footprints leading away from where she had been sleeping. For a moment panic threatened, but she reminded herself that the packs were there. He wouldn't have gone anywhere without them.

She followed the footsteps to the top of the ridge and paused as she embraced the stillness of the night around her. A noise stopped her reverie, and she turned to see Alexei as he stood in the shadows of the trees, his gaze locked on hers before he began walking toward her.

Her heart raced as he neared, the air around them thickening with anticipation. He stopped in front of her, so close that she could feel his breath on her face, and she bobbed a curtsy. When she straightened his eyes seemed to caress hers, and an inexplicable shiver ran down her spine. For the first time she felt like maybe she truly had stepped into another world, one where anything could happen.

Alexei had done his best to clear his mind and plan his next course of action, but even still he thought of her, as he had almost every moment since he had met her. He also thought of stories growing up about a mysterious magical kingdom, and when thoughts drifted back to her he wondered if he was encountering one of its secrets himself. It should matter, knowing the implications if she was a part of it, and what the punishment was for such a crime. Still, that wasn't why he didn't want her connected to any of it. He simply didn't want her to belong to anyone or anything except him, rational thoughts be damned.

He stopped short when he found her standing in a patch of moonlight surrounded by the soft light, completely unaware of how beautiful she was. Time seemed to slow as he walked toward her. He almost couldn't believe she was real. When her eyes locked on his she smiled, and his only thought was that he wanted to keep her there with him hidden amongst the shadows.

As he reached her, she curtsied, and when she lifted her head and met his eyes, he felt his heart in his throat. She straightened, and he took her hand and brought it to his lips, testing himself, testing her.

"How are you feeling?" His eyes roamed her face looking for any signs of the pain that glazed over her earlier. He was relieved to see that it was gone.

"Much better. Thank you for taking care of me."

"I'm glad."

His head inclined and she closed her eyes and waited for his lips to touch hers. She was surprised when instead they brushed her forehead lightly. She would have been disappointed, but the sweetness of the moment wouldn't allow it. When Alexei pulled back, she looked into his eyes and started to lean up, to follow his movement. His gaze flashed with heat when he realized her intent and stayed still to let her control the moment.

At that instant a deer jumped out onto the path. Neither one heard it coming because they had been too saturated in their own thoughts. They jumped apart and prepared to run, but they stopped short when they saw it was a deer, not a slew of soldiers. Their chests heaved, awkward now with the moment between them gone even though the intensity still lingered.

"Well then," he said and paused. "That was close."

From the look on his face, she couldn't tell if he was referring to the almost kiss or what could have been a sticky situation if it had been a soldier instead of a deer. It was a reminder that reality awaited them outside of that perfect moment in time.

"Why don't we get some sleep?" He took a deliberate step back. "Tomorrow is going to be another long day."

She nodded. She was a little disoriented and wished that he wouldn't have stepped back, but maybe it was for the best.

Alexei thought of what had just happened. If that had been someone, how would he have protected her? The deer had been a wake-up call for a man going under.

He needed to focus. He reached out a hand to her and when she took it, he began walking back toward their camp he had set up for the night.

"I would love to start a fire tonight, but I don't know if I want to risk it just in case the men didn't go back as planned. Them seeing the smoke is too much of a risk to take."

"So is freezing to death," she grumbled, and he gave her a quick grin, relieved that the moment had seemingly passed.

"It does get colder outside at night, but we will be okay. I brought that large blanket, and we could sleep together." She looked at him and quirked an eyebrow. "For body heat," he clarified quickly, but it was too late. He was right back on a path full of thoughts he shouldn't be having.

"That seems like a sensible plan all around." The mere thought of it warmed her from the inside out. Who needed the blanket?

She took her hair out of the band, letting it fall long and loose. He couldn't help himself and reached out to run a hand down it before he tucked a strand behind her ear.

"You need to get some sleep."

She nodded but she couldn't help but ask, "I know there are some things you are keeping to yourself for a reason, but can't you tell me anything?"

"Not much. It's more of a long bedtime story."

"It's bedtime." She sat down and patted the ground next to her. "Tell me a story."

He smiled and sat down. "Keep in mind, the story probably depends on who is telling it, but I can tell you what was told to me."

She nodded.

"There used to be magic in another kingdom, Mearan." The name hit her, and she had that feeling again, like there was something just under a layer of haze, some answer she was supposed to know.

He must not have noticed her stiffen because he kept going. "Westrim utilized knowledge as their own power, but still, it was different. The two kingdoms were never exactly chummy, but one day something made them bend toward each other. Some say friendship, some say love, but maybe they are just romanticizing the situation. Regardless, they lived amongst each other in peace for the first time." He picked up a rock and threw it.

"As they say, all good things come to an end. Conspirators on both sides stirred up trouble with whispers and lies most likely led by fear and jealousy. Every day tensions grew until the day that a horrible illness spread through Westrim. I was young, but it killed half the kingdom, including my parents. Everyone believed that it was fabricated by Mearan, their way of getting rid of the problem, so to speak."

"Did they?" she asked breathlessly.

He shrugged. "It depends on who you ask. Mearan claims that it was self-inflicted. That we people of Westrim sacrificed many for the good of the cause to gain sympathizers. There are several other regions around, not quite as powerful, but with enough people to help turn the tide if a war came. When my parents died my uncle was crowned. He tells me that it was the most difficult decision he ever made whether to push back or not. People were drowning in grief and wanted vengeance and he listened to their pleas. He was dealing with his own grief and was thrown into a role he wasn't prepared for. He was crowned as interim king until I was old enough. Now that I am twenty-one, I'm next."

He closed his eyes for a minute as if he could erase those memories. "Anyway, using the knowledge at their disposal and some borrowed magic, Westrim was able to come up with a plot to vanquish the magic for good."

"What happened?" she whispered.

"Mearan did the same. They used their magic and consulted sympathizers to help devise a protection spell. What was coming their way couldn't be stopped, so they did their best to deflect, I guess you could say. They were forced into seclusion and cast out their magic."

She mulled that over. "Do you think that is what really happened?"

"Honestly, I have no idea." There was a beat of silence between them, and he saw that she was deep in thought so he continued on, "One of my teachers once said that magic was capable of reshaping reality itself. If you think about it, it works outside natural laws and principles. That is why Westrim thought the illness was fabricated by Mearan. It certainly reshaped reality. But I'm not sure that we will ever know the truth. Without any proof it's hard to know anything for certain."

"It does seem rather unfair all around. Both sides suffered so much loss. I'm sure there is a lot missing from the story, things that you may never know."

He nodded in agreement. "I can't help but wonder what I would have done, if I would have made the wrong choice?" If there was even a right choice at all.

She thought of how the magic was hidden away, which meant it could be found, could be freed. "How can the magic be freed?"

She was so deep in her thoughts she didn't realize that he couldn't meet her eyes when he answered. "No one knows."

"And if it isn't set free?"

He shrugged. "No one has said much on that part of it. If you are up for it, I have one more story for you."

She bobbed her head absently, taking in everything he had just told her, only focusing when he took her hand in his and absently played with her fingers. She wondered if he held onto her more for his benefit or hers.

He spun a tale of how a stranger had been brought to his kingdom through a gust of wind that looked like a scatter of luminescent stars followed by a flash of bright light. It was as if a gateway had been unlocked by a powerful surge of energy that was powerful enough to pass through worlds.

"I saw it." He looked at her meaningfully. "I felt it. That wind somehow crashed into me like a wave. It went through me. And when the wind stopped and the light faded, it left something behind."

"What?" she whispered. "What was left?"

His lips curved into a gentle smile that brought warmth when not long before, after their almost kiss, there had been heat. "You," he continued. "It brought me you."

She had no idea what to make of what he had just told her, and her heart raced as she tried to process the implications of the statement. It seemed too unbelievable, but so was everything else, and she had to learn more about that mysterious moment that had changed her life forever. Finally, her thoughts landed on his words, "It brought me you." Moreso the way he said them. She wanted to ask what his words meant, but at the same time, a part of her wasn't sure if she was ready for either outcome. Best not to touch on that for now.

He waited patiently for what she was going to say and had to actively force himself not to laugh at what came out of her mouth next.

"After all of that you willingly approached me?" she asked incredulously. "Were you scared?" She knew it wasn't a very manly question to ask, but who wouldn't think twice about approaching that.

He shook his head and let out a soft laugh. "I wasn't scared. I was enchanted." He had somehow felt connected to her from that one moment in time, and every moment after. "I'm still enchanted."

She gave him a sweet, wondering smile, and he wished he could have stopped there, but he didn't want to keep more from her than he already was.

"That's not all of it. I think," he said, before he could change his mind, "that you are somehow connected to Mearan. Only that kind of power could have brought you here."

He heard her breath hitch as she stared back, wide-eyed and breathless. It felt like the world around them was standing still. He wanted so desperately to be able to read her thoughts and understand what she was feeling. To be able to step inside of her mind and provide whatever comfort she needed.

"I thought they didn't have any magic left?"

"I know it doesn't make sense. The magic was hidden away, but maybe there was some left, like a limited amount or a stockpile."

"Why would they use that up on me?"

"We will have to add that to the list of questions we will be asking."

She let out a breath in a whoosh. "Well. That is a heck of a story to tell a person right before bed."

She wished she could have laughed off his theory, but the realization that she was in what was most likely another world, another realm crashed down on her again. What had brought her there if not magic? The bigger question was still, why?

"Get some sleep," he said as if it was going to be easy after that.

She nodded and had to admit that she was too tired to take it all in, to think about it too much. It was too big, the thoughts too encompassing. Instead, she lay down and covered up with the blanket, waiting with nerves and anticipation for him to crawl in with her.

"I'll be right back," he said before he leaned down and pulled the blanket up higher around her neck. "I just want to do a quick check again."

He felt guilt creeping in knowing there was still something that he was keeping from her. How could he possibly know for sure if his suspicions were right? Why give her more uncertainty or hurt her over nothing? He stayed silent as his head and heart battled in a tug of war and told himself he would share with her when the time was right. He had said no more secrets, and hadn't kept anything new from her, just tucked away the one piece of information that could change everything.

Chapter Eleven

Ellery was tired but restless.

I can't be magic. I'm just an ordinary girl with an ordinary life.

She thought of the impossibility of her being connected to something magical. Other than her recent dreams, nothing out of the ordinary in a magical way had ever happened to her. She thought of going home and the security her real life provided. Maybe soon she would leave this world full of mystery and fall back into her routine where it was comfortable and safe. A wave of grief washed through her as she lay there wondering how much time she had left there… with Alexei. Those thoughts left a bittersweet feeling that pulled at different parts of her, and she worried that if those parts ever met, they would implode.

There was something about him that made her feel both safe and excited all at once. Though she feared what might come next, she couldn't help but be fascinated by the possibilities. She hadn't expected this kind of journey, or this kind of man, but now that both had seemingly found her, she wanted to embrace it. She wanted it to be real more than she had ever allowed herself to want anything before.

That was a problem, though. Wanting things, needing things, was a dangerous game to her. One she was afraid she was losing every time she looked at him.

She sighed and shook her head, trying to clear away the dozens of questions simultaneously buzzing around in her mind. She knew that dwelling on them now was futile. The answers would have to wait until she could make sense of it all. For now, she concentrated on the task at hand, sleep, and tried to push any overwhelming thoughts aside. Though they still lingered in the back of her mind, she was determined not to let them take over.

It wasn't until she heard his footsteps and felt him lie down behind her that she set her mind at ease knowing he was safely back with her. Sparks flew when she felt his back against her own. Even though she wished he would turn and wrap his arms around her, the pressure of his back against hers and the warmth of it steadied her. Despite everything, she fell asleep with thoughts of him on her mind.

As dawn approached, a bit of light flooded in through the trees. Ellery was still surprised to wake up there, that feeling also dueled with a sense of relief. She missed her bed and a hot shower, not to mention the thought of coffee nearly made her whimper, but all in all, she was fine. More than fine, under the circumstances.

She was stiff beyond words and decided she needed to stretch. She got up and went for a walk. She had been walking in such peace that she hadn't paid attention to where she was going and didn't realize how far she had gone. She turned to head back, not wanting to get too far away, but before she did, she smelled something. It took her a moment to realize it was smoke. Curiosity got the best of her, and she followed the scent.

As she moved in the direction her nose took her, the faint smell of burning wood grew stronger, and she saw that a pale light spilled from embers in a makeshift fire ring. It was obvious that someone had been there, and very recently. She glanced around for any movement but saw nothing. With a deep breath she stepped forward, determined to uncover whatever secrets lay around that blanket of smoke and ash.

Her eyes peered about for more details, and she saw a few half-eaten apples, a small pile of sticks, and several charred campfire remains. They had not used all the tinder. That coupled with the fact that there were still rumpled blankets, made her wonder if they were already gone and left it behind, or if they were coming back. Hard, ice blue eyes flashed across her mind.

She pushed them out of the way. Her gaze landed on something impaled in the ground. The item was slender but long, large enough that she could see it protruding out of the ground. It was a sword with half of the blade still stuck in the ground. She thought back to the soldiers the day before and recalled that some had long swords at their hips. Moreso the emblem that she had seen on Aines' vest was encrusted in the hilt of this sword.

The sword seemed to be calling out to her, the exposed blade shimmering in the sunlight as if it beckoned her forward. Although something told her to keep her distance, her curiosity won out. She cautiously stepped closer and reached out her hand to touch it. Her fingers trembled as she grazed them along the cold metal, trailing them up the blade until she grasped the hilt.

It felt heavy against her hand and before she could pull back, her hand seemed to fuse to it, like it was melding into her skin, and a searing pain flooded through her.

The pain was so unbearable that it paralyzed her with fear. She tried to take a deep breath, but the air seemed to slip away from her lips as quickly as she inhaled it. Then as abruptly as it came, the pain and pressure subsided to a dull throb and a tingling feeling that coursed through her. She clutched her hand to her chest, not being able to comprehend what happened and too terrified to look.

After a few deep breaths she mustered up the courage to look down at her hand. Her heart sank in terror when she saw a searing, red brand. The tiny emblem of the wolf was scored in the middle of her palm. She had been branded! She was incredulous, in complete and utter shock. By whom? And how, but by magic? Was it all somehow connected to the pursuit of that forbidden power?

Her thoughts raced and jumbled up her mind until nothing made sense. Before she could untangle them, she heard someone coming and walked as quickly and quietly as she could back into the trees for cover. She crouched low and tried to stay as quiet and unnoticed in the thicket as possible. Why the hell had she left that morning? She should have learned her lesson after the debacle at the cabin the day before.

She could hear footsteps coming closer, and her heart pounded faster with each step they took. Whoever it was came closer and closer until it seemed that their footsteps stopped. Suddenly she heard a noise behind her and closed her eyes. She wanted to look over her shoulder, glance at what was coming, but decided not to.

No way she could outrun whoever it was with nowhere to escape. Instead, she stilled her trembling hand with her scored palm and braced herself.

A hand covered her mouth, and she was pulled swiftly against someone before being hauled deeper into the brush. Before she had time to even try to escape Alexei turned her around to face him, then pressed a finger to his lips with his other hand to motion for quiet. She nodded and he let go. The relief of seeing him melted through her, filling every crack until there was nothing left but him.

She turned back around and sat against him and felt his chest rise and fall. It was steady, like him. That was when she heard other footsteps and a familiar voice that brought a chill that seeped into her bones. Every instinct that she had rang like alarm bells at the thought of him.

"You told me that you were following the right path? That you had tracked them." Aines' voice sounded cold and angry.

"I was. I am," the other replied, trying to sound confident.

"You better hope so."

"Another pigeon arrived this morning. We can't go back without her," she heard the other say with a touch of worry, maybe fear, in his voice. The comment also told her that they had never gone home at all.

"We won't," she heard Aines answer. She imagined a wicked grin lighting up his face when he thought of finding her and dragging her back. "We'll find her." Silence for a minute.

"Pretty little thing. I wonder what he wants with her?" It took her a moment to realize that they were referring to Alexei.

"Yeah, like that is the mystery." Aines' voice was full of sarcasm. His companion was silent in what might have been contemplation.

"Whatever she was wearing, it didn't leave much to the imagination. Maybe our lovestruck prince will share her." She heard the desire in his voice, and it made her skin crawl.

Alexei grabbed for her hand and his knuckles turned white as his grip tightened on her. His stare was filled with cold rage. She laid her other hand over his and looked into his eyes. Rage receded and he looked at her, gently laying his forehead on hers for a moment before leaning back and mouthing the word, "Never."

"It isn't his problem anymore. We will take her off his hands and do as we see fit."

"Do you really think she is one of them?"

"You saw her," Aines said matter-of-factly. "She certainly isn't one of us."

"What if she belongs to one of the other regions and not Mearan?"

"At this point it doesn't matter. She isn't one of us. That is the end of the discussion." He seemed to have thought that was the end of the conversation, but it wasn't.

"If she was magic, why wouldn't she camouflage herself? Why risk it?"

"Who knows why she is doing what she's doing. Could be arrogance. Not caring what we think, but she should," Aines said gravelly.

"What about the prince?"

"We'll deal with him, too." He sounded particularly happy about that.

"Do you think he is spellbound?"

"He had better hope so. Even being prince doesn't exclude him from treason and, it certainly looked like he was consorting with the enemy to me."

"He obviously wants to protect her, but I guess that is what he would have to do if he was spellbound."

"Like I said, he better hope so. If not, he will be in just as much trouble as her, or more."

She heard him pull the sword out of the ground, and they retreated, their steps fading away slowly until there was nothing but silence again.

The word treason spread slowly through her mind as they walked away. She may have been in a different world, but she was sure the word held the same meaning. Alexei, the crown prince, the future king of Westrim, had committed treason against the crown, himself, from the moment he met her.

And after hearing the voices of the soldiers, she knew there was no going back. He had committed himself to this path… to her. He'd gone so far as to harbor her, to openly shield her from the soldiers the king had sent to bring her back.

She was overwhelmed and confused. Why would he risk it? He would never let them hurt her, despite the personal cost.

Treason. The word turned her blood to ice. After Alexei confessed his suspicions about her ties to Mearan the night before, she knew that he knew what he was risking. He had known all along that he was disobeying the interim king by staying with her and yet, here he was. Cold dread sat against her chest as she replayed that awful word over and over.

Chapter Twelve

"**R**eally, Alexei. Treason?" She bit it out as an accusation, her voice tense and barely above a whisper, afraid the men would come running back.

Before she could question him further, he stood up and laid a hand on her shoulder indicating for her to stay there. It rankled her that he told her to stay, but she had to admit she wasn't sure she would be steady enough on her feet anyway. Before she could think anymore, he was already walking back to her, nodding to let her know the coast was clear. She tried to calm down, but it was just out of reach.

"What they said is irrelevant. It doesn't matter," he sighed heavily.

"Of course it matters. This is your life!" She looked at him in disbelief. "I don't know what it means here, but in my world, treason is pretty damn serious and so are the consequences."

"That was a law made when the kingdoms separated over a decade ago, and it shouldn't have any bearing in our world today," he explained. "Besides, nothing is black and white, not even the law that they are throwing around. Regardless of what they may think, there is always a gray area, and yes, I know how that sounds coming someone who will have almost complete authority one day. But you and I, what is happening here, is every shade of gray there is."

She wasn't sure what he meant by that, so she decided she wasn't going to touch it. "So what, are you aiding and abetting an enemy?"

He took a step closer, and she almost stepped back. "You and I both know that you're not the enemy," he said slowly and looked her in the eye. "No one is going to tell me that you are," he continued, his voice rising in volume and intensity. "If you want to believe that, then so be it, but I won't stand here and act like you are some damn threat." His gaze never left hers, and the tension between them was palpable. "You can either believe them and the crap they are spewing," he said firmly, "or you can believe that they don't know what is going on any more than we do. But one way or another, I'm going with you." He squared his shoulders and waited for her response.

"Why would you risk it?"

"You would, too," he shot back.

That was something else she also wasn't going to touch. Then she gave him a questioning look. "How did you find me?"

"I woke up, and you weren't there. I saw a few of your tracks and I followed them."

"Since you are so hellbent on being the hero, I might as well give you another problem we need to solve." She tried to push back the worry that had returned when she thought of the brand, because it felt like being pulled down by a strong current. "You might change your mind about everything when you see this. I don't know what it means, but I don't think it's good." She took a deep breath and let all her cards lay on the table as she stretched out her arm and slowly opened her fingers, showing him the brand.

It struck her again as she saw it. The crest was a beautiful design in the shape of a wolf standing tall. If she wasn't so horrified, she would have marveled at the intricate detail and how perfect the shape of it was on her skin.

"This is my family's crest," he said in a low, grave voice. "How did this happen?"

"This," she said with a smile that didn't reach her eyes, "is because curiosity killed the cat." She paused for a moment before continuing, her expression turning serious as she told him about the sword.

Alexei stared at her outstretched palm. He felt shock going through him in waves. He didn't know how to process what he was seeing. While the mark scored into her palm validated his suspicions, he realized he hadn't fully allowed himself to believe the possibility of it. Not entirely. His mind raced as he tried to make sense of everything, but no answer seemed to be forthcoming. He couldn't take his eyes off the brand, his own crest, that marred her skin.

"We'll get to the bottom of it," he said, wanting to shield her from what it meant.

Another lie to add to the list, he thought vehemently. He kept telling himself it was to protect her, but was it?

"Don't worry," he said before he took her hand gently in his and brought it up to his mouth, kissing the brand lightly. He released her hand and let his gaze linger for a minute before tearing it away.

Ellery didn't miss the way his breath caught and how he had paled when he saw the brand. She tried to read what was going on behind those instantly guarded depths, but he wouldn't meet her gaze. She would let him keep his thoughts, for now.

The whole situation put her on edge as they walked back to clean up the small camp they had set up. "We should keep going. Maybe if we follow them closely, we can stay one step ahead of them."

He shook his head adamantly but did his best to clear his face of any unwanted emotion, not wanting to betray his newfound fear for her. "I know what you are saying, but it is too risky."

She thought of everything he was risking by helping her, and she had only been thinking of getting where they needed to, not considering the danger of it all that was becoming clearer by the day.

"I'm sorry, that was a selfish thought. I know you have just as much stake in all of this now, more so, because of me."

"No, it wasn't, and I'm not worried about me. I'm worried about you. I don't want to risk running into them and me not being able to protect you. Not that I don't have faith in my skills to protect you, but even for me six of my soldiers who I know are trained to the max might be a stretch. But if you are that adamant about going let's find a way to settle it." If anyone else said that she might have thought it was arrogance, but she had a feeling he could more than handle himself in any situation.

"You mean a compromise?"

He nodded.

"I happen to have a pretty straightforward way that can fairly settle almost all disputes."

As a future ruler, that was music to his ears. "Okay, let me hear it."

"It is called rock, paper, scissors." She explained the rules.

"You have got to be kidding me," he said dryly.

His face was so serious that she giggled. She shook her head. "Can't say that I am. I have found this to be very diplomatic."

"This would save a lot of arguing at court next time." They both laughed.

"Okay, are you ready? Let's do a test run."

"Ready," he said, and she dazzled him with a grin.

He couldn't help but smile back, she was obviously pleased by his willingness to take part. Thank goodness she couldn't read minds, or she would have known that if she kept smiling at him like that there wasn't a lot he could have said "no" to.

"Rock, paper, scissors, shoot," she said as if his world hadn't just been tilted on its axis, but he forced himself to concentrate for her.

Both paper.

"Again." He took rock, and she took paper. She won.

"Okay, for real now."

"Rock, paper, scissors, shoot." He was paper, and she was rock that time.

"Beginner's luck," she said and exaggeratedly stretched out her arms and rolled her head from side to side. "I'm ready now."

"Rock, paper, scissors, shoot." She was scissors, and he was paper.

"See, more intense than you thought," she said when she caught his furrowed brow.

The last time she went with scissors again, and he was victorious with rock.

She gave him a bow. "I concede, Your Highness. Stay put it is."

"Really?" he asked skeptically, thinking there had to be a catch.

She shrugged. "You won fair and square."

"I really should implement that as an acceptable form of decision making," he said seriously and she laughed. The sound shot straight through him.

CHAPTER THIRTEEN

"What I wouldn't do for a long, hot shower," she said, and stretched her stiff, sore muscles. It had been another whole day without one.

He smiled and tried to stifle the image. "How about a cold bath instead?" he said and nodded toward the stream.

She started to laugh but saw from the look on his face that he was completely serious. She sighed inwardly. "Well, that'll have to do." Then she quit laughing when she heard something in the distance. She concentrated and realized it was music. "Did you hear that?"

He shook his head and then listened again before nodding his head. She went to walk toward it, and he put his arm out, stopping her. "Not a chance."

"We can't just walk away."

"Sure we can."

"I think if it is them, it is good to know where they are. But I didn't see any instruments on their belts, only cold hard steel. Besides, something tells me that they aren't sitting around with a fiddle like some merry band."

This time he reached for her hand and tried to pull her away. Something was telling her to keep going. Feelings inside of her started waking up, different from before. Feelings that began to ease an ache she didn't even know she had. It urged her to go.

She heard his audible sigh. "If you are so determined to do this, let me go first."

Her pride bristled. "I am not some…"

"Trust me, I know, but for once maybe let me show a bit of my chivalry off."

They would never know who would have won that battle because they heard someone walking through the underbrush toward them. He pushed her behind him and leaned down toward his boot, not taking his eyes off of the direction of the sound. She was shocked when she saw him pull something out, and she saw the glint of a knife. He kept it clutched in one hand and the other hand reached around to feel for her. She was shocked to see the knife, and grateful for it because she had nothing to protect herself with but her wits. Because of that, she reached for the hand that he held out.

The man who rounded the corner shot her an easy smile. There was no malice there, and he seemed relaxed despite the clear threat Alexei posed. His light brown hair fell in curly waves to his shoulders and framed his features which were softer than Alexei's but just as prominent. There was a certain vitality to him that made him hard to look away from.

"Good evening. A nice night out for a walk," his voice called out. Ellery smiled at the lilting accent she heard.

He had a sinewy build, and she could tell from the t-shirt that seemed to be molded to his torso that muscles rippled underneath. As he walked, there was a grace to his movements which seemed at odds with the fact that he was trudging through the woods. When he got closer, she saw the goodness emanating from his sea-green eyes. She was charmed to see that they had laugh lines at the corners. Ellery instantly felt she could trust the man.

"Where are you headed?" he asked and flashed her another grin. The quick flash of white against his sun-bronzed skin was dazzling enough to cause temporary blindness… luckily it was Alexei who spoke for them.

"We could ask the same of you," Alexei said. "What are you doing out in the middle of the forest by yourself?"

The young man rubbed a calloused hand over his lean jaw and bit the pink skin of his full bottom lip as he thought and sent Ellery a glance before looking back toward Alexei with a chiding air.

"Come on now, Your Highness. We both know that you heard the music, you know I'm not alone."

Alexei tensed and she was just as shocked as he was. She assumed at some point that they would be found out, and that someone would recognize him, but she certainly hadn't expected it to happen like this.

"Have we met before?" Alexei asked cautiously.

"I haven't had the pleasure," the young man said dryly, and Ellery was fairly certain he didn't mean it.

"You aren't from Westrim, then?" At the question something flashed in the man's eyes cold and hard and for a moment she thought she imagined it.

"No, I'm not," he said, effectively ending that conversation. He looked over Alexei's shoulder at her and gave her another smile which was definitely in contrast to how he felt about the prince standing in front of her. She wasn't entirely sure how she felt about it.

"Why don't you stop here for the night?"

"Why would we do that?"

"We have some answers that you might need. Besides, it isn't like she can make it all the way home tonight. You need somewhere to sleep."

Ellery went to move around Alexei, and his arm reached out again for her to keep her back. He raised the knife a little higher.

The handsome stranger seemed easygoing but after glancing at the knife she was sure he was on alert.

"How do we know we can trust you?" Alexei asked. The comment he made about her not being able to make it home didn't escape him, but he certainly wasn't having a discussion about it right then and there.

"There are wards around this camp. You have to meet certain… criteria to be able to make it past. That goes for anyone, myself included." He looked at Ellery again and there was interest in the depths of his gaze, but there was also more.

It was like she was an answer to a question he had been asking himself. When his gaze shifted back to Alexei that look was long gone. "Sometimes it is easier to show you than tell you."

He took a step forward and flashed a grin at Alexei. "At ease soldier. I'm not going to do anything." Then he put his hand out, and while she thought it was to show them that he didn't have a weapon, she realized that there was the same brand on his hand as on her own. Before she thought any better of it, she stepped away from Alexei, skirting his arm and offered her own hand, palm up.

"Like calls to like," he said simply.

"How did you know?" she whispered as they both stared down at the identical brand.

"Oh, we know more than you can imagine."

"We?"

"There is someone who has been waiting for you." His gaze and voice were like a soothing caress when he looked at her.

She turned and looked at Alexei who was giving her a look as if he was asking a question. She wasn't sure if he was asking her to leave or asking her thoughts. She turned and stood in front of him, those eyes looked down at her, like heavy fog in the morning. They were patient and worried when they landed on her. Although she knew he was worried for her, not himself.

"This is safe. Trust me," she said.

She was sure he wanted to do anything but go with the stranger, but he leaned down and replaced the knife before straightening and nodding at the stranger. She turned to walk but he reached for her hand and laced their fingers together.

"Well, Ellery," the young man said, his voice honey smooth. "We are happy to have you here with us tonight." His brow line was firm, and she thought it would have made him look perpetually serious, but his strong features softened when he smiled, and she couldn't help but smile back. Alexei, however, had no such compunction.

"How do you know who I am?"

"All in good time." Then she noticed when his gaze shot to Alexei that the firm brown line came back swiftly, and it didn't soften one bit until his gaze landed on her again. Either he really liked her, or really disliked him. She wasn't sure how he could have made a snap decision like that about either one of them, but at this point she wasn't going to be quick to dismiss anything.

"You somehow know both of us. What about you?" Alexei said.

The cold, flat tone was back. "I assumed this," he raised his hand and showed the brand, "told you everything that you cared to know about me?"

"What is that supposed to mean?"

"Never mind, not the time," he said as if reminding himself. "I'm Kellen."

"Nice to meet you, Kellen." She squeezed the hand holding hers.

"If something happens to her, there is no place in this world or another where you could hide," Alexei said in his own way of greeting.

The young man had the good sense to pale for a second before he flashed them both a grin. "I get it. Come with me."

The whole last couple minutes seemed to pile on so many more questions but there was no time because the music got louder. They could smell smoke, and there was laughter that rang through the trees and reached them. Ellery cautiously approached the camp, trying not to draw too much attention to herself. As she got closer, she noticed that the people in the camp seemed different from any other group she had encountered before in her dreams. There was a certain aura of mystery surrounding them.

She couldn't help but wonder about who the mysterious travelers were, and what secrets they held as they camped out in the middle of the forest. The first thing that she noticed was that there was joy there. Some were sitting by the fire, others playing music or dancing along. Kids wove in and out of the trees playing a game of tag.

As she entered the camp, they were greeted with warm smiles and friendly faces. Her eyes took in every bit of detail that she could until her eyes landed on someone sitting at the fire. Her breath caught in her throat as recognition slammed into her.

Kellen looked at her and his face lit up. "Go ahead, she's been waiting for you."

She walked toward the woman on unsteady legs, and wasn't sure why, but she fought back tears that threatened to spill over. Maybe it was because she was the first familiar thing from her real life that she had seen.

There before her Mrs. Hansen sat by a fire with a smile on her face. Even sitting there in the middle of the forest she had a subtle elegance about her. She kept her eyes on Ellery's as she made her way to her, eyes that were like the deepest blue of the sea. Subtle crow's feet and the heavy hoods of her eyelids did nothing to dull the command of her presence.

Ellery had blurry eyes from the tears, and Mrs. Hansen stood up and opened her arms for her. Without thinking, she moved into them and let someone hold her, let herself think that for a moment everything was okay. Let herself be vulnerable. That was not a normal state for her to be in. But there, in that moment, it felt right.

"There you are, sweet girl," she said and ran a hand down the long braid Ellery had put in her hair that morning. "I wondered when you would make it to me."

"Mrs. Hansen?" she said with a question in her voice.

"Yes, it's me," the kindly woman said and released Ellery, holding her at arm's length to look at her as if inspecting for any bumps and bruises. "Although here I go by Clara."

Then she looked over her shoulder, and Ellery followed her stare to a furious Alexei still across the camp standing beside Kellen. She assumed Kellen told him to give them a minute or he would have been right beside her, she was sure of it.

"Your young man is very protective of you."

"He's not," she said too quickly but nothing more because she cut herself off. Not what? Not protective… that was a lie. Not hers?

That felt like a lie too when everything inside of her told her otherwise. Instead, she left it at that and turned back around.

The woman gave her a knowing smile before motioning for him to come. "Let's bring him over so you both can hear this all at once. I'm sure you have plenty of questions."

"You have no idea," Ellery said, still trying to let her mind catch up with everything that had just happened. She sat down on a log that was closest to her. Clara nodded her head toward the two men who walked toward them.

Alexei stood next to where she sat and looked down at her. She looked up and smiled. Despite his irritation she could sense just below the surface that his eyes softened on hers. "Are you okay?" he asked.

She nodded. "I'm fine. Alexei, this is Mrs. Hansen. I mean Clara. My neighbor." That sounded ridiculous even to her own ears, but it was true. It just seemed so normal, introducing her as her neighbor.

He turned and bowed his head to her. "It is nice to meet you, Clara. I'm—"

"Oh, I know who you are, Prince Alexei."

If he was shocked by that, he covered it up well. "Please, call me Alexei or Alex."

She smiled at that. "It is nice to have you here with us, Alexei. Please sit. We can eat and then I'm sure we have much to talk about."

CHAPTER FOURTEEN

They ate in relative quiet with only the music and merriment behind them. When they were done, they all turned their heads to Clara expectantly.

"How are you here?" Ellery blurted out. "Are you from here, or are you from there? How is this possible? Did you bring me here?" Then she felt her cheeks heat as she realized she had just spouted off. Alexei reached around her and put his hand on her lower back rubbing circular motions on it to try to soothe her. She wanted to snap that she didn't need to be coddled, but the touch, the support, felt too good.

"Let me start by saying that I'm going to answer as many questions as I can."

"What do you mean that you *can*?" Alexei asked.

She ignored that and looked toward Ellery. "What all has he told you so far?"

Ellery assumed it was about their conversation the night before, and she relayed what he had told her about the two kingdoms.

In response Clara lifted her hand and showed them the brand there. She briefly looked to Ellery. "It was glamoured in your world."

"I'm assuming you have an idea of what this is?" Clara asked Alexei.

He was silent for a minute, probably choked from the weight of the stare Ellery threw at him. "Not much more than an idea."

Kellen scoffed on the other side of the fire where he sat. Alexei's jaw ticked but he ignored him. "I know that there are ways to mark people who have magic in the blood. I'm assuming this is how." Ellery settled at that. He had kept that piece of information from her, but even he didn't know the entirety of it.

Clara looked at Ellery. "I have magic, as does Kellen, and you as well." Then she spread her hand out across the camp. "Some others do, but many do not."

"Why the brand, why do they want to know who all is magic? If the tale is true then it is locked up, right?"

"In a way. For those who are sequestered in Mearan it is locked up, waiting, but not everyone was there when the spell was put over the kingdom. I know how fond you are of stories, and I wish I could tell you this whole story. One day I will, but for now I'm going to tell you everything that I can."

"A long time ago, a little girl was sent to another world because of a prophesy. Her parents knew that in time what was prophesized would come to pass and many things would be lost. Friendships, lives, magic. When the time came, nothing would be able to stop it. But there was hope in the darkness of the prophesy—someone would be able to set things to right. Not wanting to take chances on the one thing that would be able to save them all, they did the hardest thing that they ever had to do and sent her away hoping that when the right time came, she would save her kingdom and bring back the magic. She was the key to saving them all."

Silence had fallen over the camp. The only thing that Ellery heard was the crackle of the fire. Clara gave a pointed look over her shoulder, and the music and chatter started back up. Ellery hadn't even realized it had stopped. She wasn't entirely sure that she was breathing. The implications were too much to take in.

"You said 'she,'" Alexei said from beside her in little more than a whisper.

"I did."

"And you think that is Ellery?"

Clara looked at him and shook her head. "I've already said too much." Then she looked to Ellery with a smile that seemed a little sad. "Everything you need is inside of you."

"So that's it? That's all you can tell her?" Alexei said and sounded angry, probably because the thing he feared was actually coming to pass right before his eyes, and he wouldn't be able to save her from it. He hadn't truly allowed himself to believe that was true.

"There wouldn't be anything to tell if it weren't for your precious kingdom," Kellen shot out.

"That's not fair, Kellen," Clara said, and she meant it. "There are two sides to every story, and you know it."

"I might have been just a boy, but I remember my side of the story."

Ellery ignored all of it and focused on Clara. "How did you both get out?"

"I was already out," Kellen answered first with anger still edging his voice. "The fight may have been between the two kingdoms, but it affected everyone, all of the smaller regions. My family was influential in Mearan, and they were sent to the different regions to try and gain support. What was coming may have been inevitable, but we had to try."

"What happened?"

He shot a look at Alexei. "Westrim soldiers came. They held everyone hostage as they weeded people out."

"What do you mean?"

He held out his hand. "Those of us who had magic in the blood were branded."

Silence.

"We were separated and taken away. Our caravan was ambushed and many of us were saved. I tried to find my parents but I didn't see them anywhere, and we didn't have a lot of time. I'm assuming they were killed… isn't that what happens to traitors?" he said bitterly.

She looked to Clara. "Did you save him?" Clara nodded. "And you have been here the whole time?"

"That was over ten years ago. We haven't just been here. We moved around a lot."

She thought of the timing of things. It couldn't be her who was meant to save them then. The timing didn't add up. That was ten years ago, and she was twenty-one. Then she remembered her saying that there had been a prophesy long before it all came to pass. Still, not possible, she thought. It had to have been wrong.

"Will you ever be able to stop running?"

"Yes, when the magic is set free."

She had left the biggest question for last. Although there were many more, she knew this was the one that mattered.

"How?"

This time Clara knew what she meant.

"I had been tasked with keeping an eye on you. Some of us have the magic to cross barriers. It is rare, but it can be done. I am one of the ones with the ability to cross between the worlds. I was there when the spell took place and was able to leave to help others that had been taken." Then she looked over at Kellen with a smile. "Ever since then I had a foothold in both worlds. I was able to be here, but also able to keep an eye on you there."

"The music that night at the apartment?" she asked.

Clara called one of the children over and whispered in his ear. He went over to where a group of people were playing the instruments, and the melody that had been playing in her apartment started.

"It was time. I tried to nudge you a bit to prepare you for what was happening."

"So you brought me here?"

She nodded.

"Can you send her back?" Alexei asked beside her. "She isn't safe here."

"That is out of my hands. When she has completed what she needs to, she will have the option to stay or go."

"Why weren't you there when I woke up?"

"Like I said, there is only so much that I can do, can say. You know everything that I can tell you for now. I wish I could tell you more, do more, but it is up to you. *Both* of you," she emphasized as if there was meaning to the word.

"It wasn't a coincidence that Alexei was the one who found me?"

"I can't say one way or the other, but I do know that fate helps us get on the right path."

She wasn't ready to unpack all of that, so she moved on. "Until it is free, those who were at the kingdom when the spell was cast are trapped there?"

She nodded. "It may be home, but there is no freedom in it."

Out of the corner of her eye she caught the look that Kellen shot Alexei again, and she instinctively scooted closer to him.

"From what I can tell it's not his fault any more than it is yours, Kellen." Ellery had to admit that while she was a bit irritated that Alexei hadn't mentioned what he assumed about the brand, he had done everything to keep her safe. "He was just a kid, too, and if I remember the story correctly, he lost his parents as well. Whatever happened, he isn't to blame any more than you are."

She felt Alexei's gaze on her, but she didn't look over. She had so many feelings crowding her mind. A tap on her shoulder saved her from having to deal with the rest of them. She turned around and saw a few of the little girls bouncing on their toes.

"We made something for you, miss," one said with blonde curls and big blue eyes. She couldn't have been older than five.

Ellery melted. "You made something just for me?"

They nodded. "Close your eyes. It's a surprise."

She leaned in and closed her eyes. She opened one slightly, teasing them and they giggled. "No peeking!" one squealed.

"Okay." She nodded and crossed her heart before closing them again.

She felt something placed on her head. "Open them!"

She opened her eyes. "Can I see it?" They nodded. She took it off and saw that it was a crown made of daisies and ferns. It was beautiful. When she put it back on, she smiled at the girls.

"Thank you, it is beautiful. I feel like a princess."

She was looking at the little girls and didn't realize that Kellen and Clara exchanged a look at that.

"Come play with us," they all chimed in, still bouncing on their toes from excitement. Ellery looked over to the rest of them. There was laughter in her eyes, and Alexei could tell that she genuinely wanted to go. They all nodded for her to go, and in less than a minute she was somehow wrapped up in a game of hide and seek.

He heard Kellen clear his throat. If he said anything Alexei hadn't heard. He only had eyes for her. Reluctantly he turned back to the man across from him who had been looking at him like he wanted nothing more than to take his head off. He could try, Alexei thought. He wasn't some pampered prince, and if he kept sneering at him in between sneaking glances at Ellery he was going to find that out really soon. Which was why he was surprised when Kellen leaned in a bit and seemed to concentrate on what he was going to say next.

"Obviously, we have more to learn about each other than I thought."

Alexei nodded in agreement. "I had no idea what happened back then, what they did to you, and your family. Everyone."

Clara scoffed, "Of course you didn't. You were just a child. What counts is how you handle things now. That crown is soon going to be weighing heavy on your head. I guess we'll see what decisions you make then. Right, Kellen?" She shot him a look, and he lifted his hands in surrender.

"You are both good boys, and she is going to need both of you for what is in store for her, so you better learn how to work together for her sake."

Alexei wanted to say that they didn't need a damn thing from Kellen, and that he would take care of her himself, but something told him that he needed to get to the bottom of it first for her sake. Before he could say anything, laughter reached his ears, sweet unguarded laughter. He turned to see Ellery pulled into a dance with the kids and instantly wanted to be with her. Before he could stand to join Kellen beat him to it.

"Excuse me, Clara." Kellen gave a wolfish grin that set Alexei's teeth on edge. "I have a sudden urge to dance."

"Have a good time, dear. I have a handsome prince to keep me company, but maybe you could stoke the fire a bit before you go."

Alexei looked for something to stoke it with himself but was shocked when Kellen simply lifted his hand and what was a dying fire flared back to life. Then Kellen gave him a smirk and walked toward the dancers.

He would have had a retort, but he was still trying to process what had just happened. He gaped at the fire, jaw dropped before he snapped it shut. Alexei knew that Kellen was magic, the brand said as much, but to see it with his own two eyes was something entirely different. He had never felt so out of place before in his whole life.

He saw that Clara's eyes twinkled with amusement before he turned back to Ellery. The music picked up and when Kellen got closer, he reached out a hand and at the same moment he saw leaves kick up and swirl around her as if she was standing in a gust of wind. She looked around in shock before looking to Kellen, her eyes wide. He moved his hand again and the wind seemed to swirl at her back and pushed her toward him.

"Convenient," Alexei muttered.

He watched as Kellen caught her up against his chest and spun her around, leading her in a quick dance. He turned her in another spin and when he pulled her back into him, he used his other hand and sent another gust of wind toward the kids. Leaves swirled around and created a whirlwind of color. The kids took off jumping around and trying to catch them all like it was a game.

"You care about her." He heard Clara say from behind him.

He nodded. "I do."

"That's good. She's going to need you."

"What can I do?"

She shook her head. He knew he was beating at a wall, but he had to try.

"She is important, isn't she? To all of us."

"She certainly is," Clara said.

"Then help me to help her."

"I really wish I could do more. That little bit of knowledge was all I was allowed to give apart from getting her here."

"How many people can cross the barriers like that?"

"Not many, and even less can take someone with them. I might be the last."

There was a question that seemed caught in his throat, but he had to get it out. "What does my uncle know about all of this?"

She took her time, and he could tell she was trying to think of what to say. "I'm not sure what he knows. What I do know is he is a good king, but who he is as a man, I guess we will see."

He guessed that was all he was going to get out of her on that front, and it certainly gave him something to ponder over later.

"Can you at least tell me if I'm heading in the right direction by taking her there?" She stayed silent. "Not to mention how I'm going to get her through whatever spell they have around the city isolating themselves." Still silence. He sighed.

"Can you at least tell me more about her? Not about what she is supposed to do, about who she is."

"Now that I can do. I watched her most of her life." She smiled as if thinking of sweet memories before nodding to her as she danced to another song. "She hasn't had enough fun in her life."

The thought of it made his face fall. "Don't you dare let her see you look at her like that. Our girl is strong. Sometimes she had to be too strong, and that comes with a bit of pride that can get bruised."

"Oh, I believe that."

"She deserves some of the load taken from her."

"What else can you tell me?"

"She is beautiful inside and out. She is nice to everyone else, but not always to herself. She is practical but fanciful. Intelligent and independent. As she got older, she finally started to get more comfortable in who she was, is. She can be stubborn, is extremely brave." Then Clara looked at him in the eyes and held his gaze. "And she is so deserving of love."

"Are there any who have noticed how deserving of love she is?"

"Plenty have noticed." She nodded toward her, and they both looked. "And how could they not? But none that have ever turned her head." It was as if Ellery knew they were talking about her, and she turned to look at them, locking eyes with him and sending him a brilliant smile that stopped his heart.

"Looks like she finally has her eyes on someone who just might deserve it, and her."

His head snapped toward Clara, and before he was able to say anything he heard giggling behind him and saw her smile over his shoulder.

"Excuse us, Your Highness," a small voice said. He turned around to see the same golden-curled blue-eyed little girl. She was holding a crown that matched Ellery's.

"Is that for me?"

She nodded. He bowed his head and let her put it on.

"Thank you."

A chorus of your welcomes rang out, and she reached for his hand. He turned around.

"Go, dance," Clara said. "Set your worries aside for the night. You are with friends."

Another song started, and he had quickly been designated the head twirler because they took turns being twirled by him. He could see the joy there, the real happiness, in this place where he would have least expected it. So he took Clara's advice and let go.

When the music turned slow, he looked for Ellery. Spotting her, he walked over, and when she turned around her eyes stared up into his.

He smiled at her softly with a question in his eyes as if he was deciding something. "Dance with me."

She let out a nervous laugh. "You might want to lower your expectations. Not all of us grew up dancing at balls."

She was right, of course. He had danced at plenty of balls with beautiful women in beautiful gowns, but none of it compared to that moment.

"I'll lead," he said gently and reached out a hand to her.

CHAPTER FIFTEEN

It was more than just a dance, and the weight of that thought had her frozen.

"Ellery," he murmured, and it sounded like a question.

Though she worried it would be a mistake, she put her hand in his. He reached for her other hand and lifted it to rest on his shoulder, giving it a reassuring squeeze before letting go. When he wrapped his arm around her, he flattened his palm on her back. As he began to hum the ballad that they were playing he led her in what she could tell was a waltz.

As she had assumed, he was an incredible dancer. He only broke the hum to whisper instructions. She felt the warmth of his breath against her ear as he spoke, guiding her through each step. His gentle voice and firm hands were a reassuring presence as she struggled to remember the instructions he had so quietly whispered in her ear because thoughts of him muddled her brain. Once she finally got the hang of it, their steps began to move in seamless harmony, as if they had been dancing together for years. It felt like one of her dreams, she thought vaguely. Not altogether real.

When the music ended, he slowed them to a stop. She looked up, and her breath hitched at the desire that stared back at her from his gaze. Heat and hunger swirled in those eyes, and she wanted to get lost in it, in that heat, and sate that hunger with him. Before she was able to do anything she felt something, then she realized someone was pulling his arm away from her.

The little girl from earlier who she learned was named Annabelle tugged at him.

"I'm next, I'm next!" It seemed that no one was immune to the handsome prince who had stolen her senses.

He gave Ellery a last searing look before the next song started and he set off dancing with the child around the forest floor. Ellery sat by the fire with Clara and watched as he danced with all of them. When the music stopped for the night, they all clamored around him, and he looked up laughing and met her eyes. That heat from earlier had turned into an inferno that she was desperately trying to put out as they were surrounded by dozens of people. She felt a hand on her shoulder and turned around to look up at Kellen.

"We have a few extra tents, and I put two up, side by side. I'm sure he isn't going to let you out of his sight."

"I don't know what has gone on between the kingdoms and what happened in the past, but the man he has become has been nothing but kind to me."

"It seems that way." He nodded in agreement. "It looks like I need to hold some more of my opinions about him until later when I get to know him more." He paused and looked in the distance. "He isn't the only one that I would like to get to know more. At some point, when the time is right, I have a story of my own to tell you." She went to ask, and he pressed a finger to her lips. His smile was so bittersweet it made her ache for him. "One day."

She told Clara goodnight, and he walked her over toward the tent. She crawled in and was just covering up when Alexei poked his head in. "Can I come in a minute?"

She nodded. "I can't believe that pack let you out of their sight. You made their night. It's not every day a prince sweeps you off your feet. I have to admit, I quite enjoyed the experience myself."

He had crawled in and sat beside her. He pushed her hair behind her ear. She wanted to tell him not to stop but she didn't have to. He stayed where he was and played with her hair, soothing her. She looked up, and she could tell he was deep in thought as he absently toyed with the smooth locks.

"What's wrong?" she asked.

"They are happy, and I am glad, but I can't help but wonder if they are forced to live like this because of me, my kingdom at least."

"You had nothing to do with this. You were a kid."

"What about now?"

"You will figure it out."

"I know he had to make some tough decisions, but no one ever said anything about what Kellen claimed. That they essentially ransacked the regions. But why would he lie about it? I can't reconcile the uncle, the man, I know with what I just heard tonight."

"When this happened he was younger, too?"

"The age that we are now," he confirmed.

"Don't forget that. Like Clara said there are two sides to every story. When is anyone completely right or wrong? I'm sure there is a lot more to it."

She could tell from the bothered look on his face that he didn't believe it, so she changed the subject. "There is one thing that is bothering me."

"What is that?"

"The story tonight was a reminder of the conversation about treason this morning, quite a reminder that we are supposed to be mortal enemies."

His hand stopped in her hair and made its way to her face. He traced from her temple down her cheek, along her jaw and then up to her lip where he ran the pad of his thumb across it. She couldn't stop a shudder.

"Does it feel like we are enemies?" he whispered, low and seductive. She thought of her books and realized they were taking the enemies-to-lovers trope to a very realistic level. He quirked his eyebrow at her. He could tell she was thinking something but since she didn't want to say the term enemy again, or lover, she kept her mouth shut. His finger stopped and before he could pull away she grabbed at his wrist and pressed a kiss to his hand, nipping his knuckle a bit. She made a decision in that moment and tugged at him to lie down with her. The next day would bring enough problems of its own but for that night, she wanted to forget about all of it.

"Knock, knock."

She recognized Kellen's voice. Alexei let out something that sounded like a growl, and she turned her head into her pillow and tried not to laugh. Not that she was thrilled with the interruption but something about the culmination of all of it heightened her emotions.

Before they said anything he peeked his head in, and she turned to look at him. He looked almost boyish and was handsome with his curly hair and smiling eyes. It was like he knew what he was doing and was more than happy to irritate Alexei in any way possible.

"Just the man I was looking for. I need to talk to you."

Alexei looked back at her and that look made her quit laughing. She sucked in a breath before clearing her throat.

"Can't it wait?" Alexei practically ground out.

"I'm not sure how much time we'll have to talk tomorrow, so I would rather have this conversation now. I'm going to go put the fire out and check on a few things. I'll be back in a couple minutes. Don't worry, I won't be long."

The look Alexei gave him would have withered a lesser man. Instead, he flashed her a grin and a wink and snickered as he closed the front of the tent.

Alexei groaned and she leaned up. This time she put her hand on his cheek and there was a bit of silence between them. They both knew why she had been drawing him down to her, and that moment still sat between them. She wanted to lean in still, kiss him and pull him to her and forget the rest of the world.

But across the camp she heard Kellen yell goodnight to the others. She assumed he would be back any minute. It was like he had put a pinhole in the tension that had been so thick. Now it was slowly leaking out.

"Better not," he said, and she stared at his mouth.

She pulled her bottom lip in and scraped her teeth against it. "Why not?"

"Because if I kiss you and he comes back, I might very literally strangle him. Besides, I don't want to be thinking of anyone else when I finally get to kiss you."

He was still sitting, leaning back on his heels and she crawled into his lap, straddling it before leaning in and whispering in his ear. "I can make you forget all about him."

He raised his arms and disappointment flooded through her when she thought he was going to lift her away, instead he put his arms around her and cupped the swell of her backside, holding her in place.

"I have no doubt." His voice came out husky.

She nipped his earlobe and started kissing along his jaw. His fingers dug into her curves where he held her, and her blood turned to fire. When both of their breaths came out quick and shallow, she leaned back and looked at him. The light that had come from her fingertips, that she had held in her hand, felt like nothing compared to what was flowing through her now. It was like that light was inside her this time and was filling every inch of her. Like she had been knotted up and twisted inside and every second that was passing was easing an ache she didn't know she had. It was intoxicating, but still, not as intoxicating as him. "Alexei," she breathed, and cupped his face before leaning in.

"I'm ready for that talk." They heard the voice from outside. Neither had heard him coming because they were so wrapped up in the moment. It was so unexpected it startled her, and she scrambled off Alexei's lap.

She watched as Alexei squeezed his eyes shut. She couldn't imagine what he was thinking, but she was pretty positive he muttered something along the lines of, no wonder they cursed his people.

"You might as well go," she said still trying to even out her voice. It was shaky even to her own ears. "He isn't going to leave."

"I could make him leave."

"You could, but something tells me he would come back anyway."

"You are probably right."

She lay back down, and he covered her up. He lifted his hand like he was going to touch her but thought better of it and pulled it back. "I'll see you in the morning. I'm in the tent right next to you if you need me."

She nodded and when he turned to give her one last look before he left the tent, she wanted to tell him to come back when they were done. But she reminded herself that they were in the middle of camp, and she had almost thrown him around like a hacky sack with a couple dozen people sleeping nearby.

"Oh my," she said out loud and wondered how she was ever going to sleep after all of that. But surprisingly the day must have gotten the better of her and she did just that.

When he left the tent Kellen was leaning against a tree, eyes lit with laughter. "I'm sorry, was I interrupting?"

He knew exactly what he had been interrupting and Alexei wanted to take all of that pent-up energy and emotion he had and use it to knock that smirk off his face, but since that wasn't an option, he kept his hands to himself. "What was so important that you had to pull me away?"

"I walk the perimeter of the wards every night to check on things."

Instinctively Alexei looked back at the tent and Kellen followed his gaze. "She is fine, everyone is. It's just a habit. Clara did the wards herself and barriers are her specialty. You couldn't be safer. Walk with me."

When Kellen pushed off the tree Alexei fell into step beside him. "Are you sure this isn't an excuse to off me and leave me in the woods for dead?"

"Tempting, trust me. I have to admit if you had presented me with that opportunity a few hours ago it would have held some appeal to me."

"And now?"

"I'm working on it. But old habits die hard. I have felt a certain way and followed along with one narrative for a long time."

Despite the fact that he just told him he would have happily left him for dead, Alexei appreciated his honesty. Most people told him what he wanted to hear. It was refreshing to be around people who weren't doing that. Under other circumstances he would be someone he wouldn't mind having around.

"I'm doing my best to remember that you were a kid too, and that you lost your parents too. You have just as much reason to hate me, but clearly your issues haven't run as deep as mine. You haven't shown anything but respect, and *affection,* for Ellery despite the fact that she is one of us."

"Honestly, I have only had one narrative too, but I know it didn't happen as badly for me after the banishment the way it did you. I didn't know about the raids and the branding. The constant hiding. I always thought the magic was locked up, and that was the end of it, unless, of course, it was released."

They both sat in silence at that statement, and while Alexei didn't want to implicate himself, he decided to follow his lead and be honest.

"It seems I have been sheltered from that, and now I'm wondering why, what the reason for it was. I also wonder if anyone would have told me if Ellery had never shown up. I'm grateful that she did, and that she has opened my eyes to see the big picture."

"She really is something," Kellen said from beside him.

"She is," he agreed but didn't say anything else. He didn't want Kellen to think about her period.

"I wish I had more time with her, but I know you need to keep going in the morning."

Alexei wondered where the conversation was heading, certainly not where he wanted, and the thought irritated him.

"Relax, lover boy, don't give me that murderous look. It's not like I'm going to go ravage her in the middle of the night. I just want to get to know her a bit."

Alexei didn't want to hear the word ravage come out of the man's mouth when he was talking about her. This time his fists tensed at his side.

"I can't help but be curious about her. If she is who I think she is, I have wondered about her for most of my life."

That time Alexei stopped walking and looked at him.

"And why is that?"

"Let's just say had things been different…" he trailed off, "but they weren't, and here we are."

What the hell was that supposed to mean? "What would have been different?"

"It doesn't matter."

"It seems like it does."

Kellen kept walking and didn't expand on it, effectively terminating the conversation with so much clearly left unsaid.

By the time their conversation was done they had made a circle and were back at Alexei's tent. He tried his best to sleep that night but thoughts of her, and what Kellen meant by that comment, kept creeping in.

Chapter Sixteen

Alexei successfully swooped Ellery out of the camp early the next morning under the guise of them needing to get on their way. He had checked the map the night before when he couldn't sleep, and he knew that they were getting close.

"We are probably no more than a day away, two at the longest. Let's head back toward the water and follow the stream for the day."

Her smile faded at that. He thought it was because they were still a day or two away, and she was eager to get back. When in reality she felt time closing in. As they walked, she decided that staying there for the day and spending more time with him was better after all. Then her thoughts turned toward the last couple days, and a feeling of helplessness took over her. He saw her concentrating, and she looked upset.

"What's wrong?"

She gave him a baleful look. "I can't get the feeling out of my head that I am helpless, and I can assure you that is a feeling that I do my best to never feel. I can't protect myself like I should," she bit out. "I can outwit people, sure, and defend myself a bit, but how far is that going to get me here, really? Will you help me?"

"Always."

"I need you to show me how to protect myself."

"I will protect you," he said.

"I'm not questioning whether or not you can or you will. I know that, but I want to be able to help myself."

He understood that and wasn't about to get into a fight over it. "When do you want to start?"

She dropped her pack. "Right now."

There was obviously no stopping her, so he nodded in agreement. He had to admit after the night before and how much the seriousness of the situation struck him, it was overdue for her to learn a few things. "Now it is. Why don't we stretch out first?"

They found a soft patch of grass to stretch in, and she decided to do some yoga. It would also help to calm her down. Alexei turned around to ask her something and his mouth went dry. His eyes followed her every movement as she contorted herself in some unnamed position. He tried his best to look at anything else, but his gaze kept drifting back toward her. He was fascinated by the curves of her body as they moved gracefully in and out of each pose. Her dark braid hung over her shoulder, and he felt his fingers practically twitch from wanting to touch her. She looked over at him, and his heart skipped a beat as their gazes met. He forced himself to look away and finish his own stretches until she was done.

When she walked back over toward him, he did his best to clear his mind. "Are you ready?"

"As I'll ever be."

"First, I'll show you a few moves for if someone is coming at you, a simple punch and kick, and how to deflect. After, I can show you a few if they actually get ahold of you." She nodded and went to stand right in front of him.

"Make sure you always steady yourself the best that you can. If you don't keep your balance, it won't end well," he said. "See that foot? Place it shoulder-width apart."

He nodded approvingly. "Now, bend your knees slightly."

He had to fight back a grin when she over-bent, and it looked like she was doing a squat. She was so focused and determined to get it right that he didn't dare laugh. If he embarrassed her, he would never be able to get her to work on it. And she was right, he needed to teach her a few things. She should know some basic moves to protect herself, even to take the knowledge back with her when she went home.

"May I?" he asked as he reached out his hands for her. He figured it would be easier to show her. Not to mention, a hands-on lesson was certainly not a hardship. She nodded.

Once she was adjusted properly, he showed her what to do with her hands and how to tuck her thumb so she didn't break her own finger in the process. Then he guided her arm in an arc, showing her how to create power with every punch she threw. She nodded and tensed her muscles as he guided her arm in an arc and into one powerful motion through the movements of a punch.

"Make sure that you keep your wrists firm," he said. "And when you hit your target, put your weight into it."

She nodded, focusing intently on his instructions as she practiced the motion over and over again. He lifted his hands and told her to hit them. She was hesitant. "You aren't going to hurt me."

The first few punches felt ordinary until she felt a bit more comfortable. But then, she started to focus on her energy and her punches had more weight behind them.

When he saw that she was comfortable with that he moved on. "The same principle applies to kicks." He showed her and then watched as she kicked forward with a little shout like she saw in the movies. He couldn't help but laugh. Who would have thought that something this simple could be so fun? He shook his head with a grin when she did it again before moving on. As with the punches, he worked with her until it became more comfortable.

"Now, you must defend yourself if someone is throwing the punches and kicks at you." As with the punch and the kick, he showed her as he explained it to her. "With your stance, you can move around fluidly, dodging what they throw at you."

He showed her how to deflect for a while before they both stilled, and she waited for what came next. They stood across from each other, and she wanted to reach out and touch the hard lines of his cheeks and trace the edges of his face along his jaw. The desire coursed through her veins, and she needed to extinguish it like a fire. She took a deep breath as he stepped closer to her until they were standing toe to toe, both of them searching each other's eyes for a moment.

His gray eyes were bright with a slight smile, but he said nothing. He lifted his hand and then put it back down at his side as if thinking better of something.

"I don't want to overwhelm you, but I would like to show you one more move. If they are coming at you from the front there is a good chance you will have time to react, but if they sneak up behind you and take hold, that is a different story. You will want to know how to break a hold."

He moved to stand behind her. "I'm going to put my arms around you in a tight hold." She readied herself, and when his arms went tight around her, they stood like that for a second. She couldn't help but tremble when she felt him pressed close against her. The desire she had tried to hold back creeped back in.

He turned her around and lifted his hand to cup her cheek. She never expected a prince to have such rough hands. She imagined they would be soft and smooth, but as a callus brushed against the sensitive skin of her cheek, she forced herself not to shiver again.

"Don't be scared." He looked into her eyes. "I would never hurt you."

"I'm fine. I promise," she said and watched as he searched her face before she turned around and pressed her back to him again. "It was just disconcerting for a moment, but getting attacked would be too." She didn't want to tell him that the shiver was from something else entirely.

"Brace yourself and make sure your feet are firmly on the ground. When you are sure you have a secure stance, shove your hips backward and lean forward. Your attacker will follow the motion on instinct and lean over you. That will cause him to lose his balance. When he does, swing to the side and turn back around quickly to knee him in the groin." He was thoughtful for a moment. "Or a punch will do just as well. If delivered properly either will certainly stop them in their tracks. Let's try it again."

This time she was more comfortable, knowing the moves that she would need to make and let herself relax. When he stepped up to her, she took a deep breath and tried not to concentrate on how good he felt there, how right she felt against him. But she couldn't think of anything but, and as it did before, it was like things that kinked up inside of her began to unravel. It felt so good, like losing a breath you had been holding. Tension she didn't even know she had was there.

"Ellery." She heard him whisper into her ear, and when she opened her eyes, she saw the little ball of energy back. It shocked her out of her reverie and again it disappeared.

What the hell? she thought to herself in frustration. Why was she malfunctioning on top of everything else?

"What were you feeling?"

She looked at him questioningly.

"Each time you started to feel the magic inside of you, even when you weren't sure what it was."

She thought about it, and it made sense that something could be connecting them together. She thought back and at first couldn't tie anything together but then realized she had been feeling a surge of emotions. Fear, anger, confusion, and the one that had broken through the strongest was desire. Desire for him. Was he the key or was it the feeling that made her magic so much stronger? Only one way to find out.

She looked at him. "It was when my emotions were heightened."

"What were you feeling right now. We can recreate it. Fear? From having to fight?" he wondered.

She slowly shook her head.

"Confusion?"

She shook her head again and looked at him in the eyes. "Last night in the tent I felt the power taking shape in a different way. It felt like something inside of me was loosening, preparing to let it free. It was coming on fast and strong, and I wasn't sure I would be able to contain it."

"Then what happened?" he said in a voice just above a whisper.

"Kellen came." She saw the moment it clicked in his head, what she had been feeling in that moment that it felt strongest. What she had obviously felt when she had just spurred it to life. "Desire," she said simply and let him see that desire in her eyes. What she felt for him was no ordinary wanting. It was strong and all consuming.

He kept his eyes on her as he moved toward her and then slowly turned her. She felt him step up to her until she could feel him against her back. There was that warmth again, that tingle that had been creeping up on her the last few days. But this time she didn't know if it was the power, or how she felt about him and what he did to her. He wrapped his arm around her waist and pulled her back firmly against his chest and in that moment she realized that she didn't care.

With the other hand he ran his hand up her side, over the side of her breast, up to trace her collarbone and then up to cup her chin as he tipped her head back and leaned down to press a kiss to her neck. He nipped his way up and before he touched her lips, her half-lidded eyes that had been full of desire lit up with pure joy as she felt the power build up. The things she felt for him radiated from her as much as the power itself.

Her heart raced faster than a shooting star in the night sky as she reached out her hand and touched the light. She felt an electric current surge through her body, a feeling of power that made her jump. This newfound energy radiated from her fingertips. As it hovered, she clasped her hands together and envisioned another one. To her delight, it was there, and she slowly raised it alongside the other one.

She tried for one more, and after a moment she had three luminescent balls of energy floating in front of her. She wondered what she could do with them, but although she was new at it, she figured she shouldn't use something until she understood it. Who knew what the power was capable of.

"That's my girl," praised Alexei.

His grip on her tightened and then he released her. She watched as the energy balls danced before them. She stood in awed silence before glancing excited eyes to Alexei.

"We did that," she said.

He offered her a grin. "You did that."

"I want to do more." Her statement hung in the air between them. As new doors of her magic were opening, what would that mean for their future… together?

CHAPTER SEVENTEEN

"If it isn't my favorite fugitive."

"Bryn?" Alexei whipped around at the voice and even as he said it, a young man pushed off a tree and sauntered toward them.

He was tall like Alexei, but brawny. His black uniform looked striking against his deep bronze skin and short, curly black hair. When he got closer Ellery saw that his smile stood out from the light stubble tracing his mouth. But it was the roughish glint in his large, dark eyes that really caught her attention.

He made quite the picture. She had to wonder what in the world they fed these men there, or what was in the water. It was as if this world cornered the market on incredibly hot men.

I wish Lily were here to see this, Ellery thought with a pang of sadness in her heart. By now her friend had probably figured out Ellery wasn't coming back to work any time soon. She wondered if she would miss her, or if her life would go on as if nothing had changed.

Bryn stopped walking toward them, eyes wide for a moment before his face went back to wearing a mask of easy charm. "Well, that certainly takes care of some unanswered questions."

At first, she assumed that he meant the brand, but quickly realized he wasn't staring at that, he was staring at the trio of light balls that was still hovering in front of her. The feeling she had that made the magic began dimming inside of her when she lost her focus. It felt like it was knotting back up inside. It was like she just needed a final push to break free of whatever constraints were holding her back from setting her magic free. Because before Alexei even turned back around to look at her the energy balls were already gone.

"It's okay, I promise," Alexei said as he tucked her into his side, keeping his arm around her in a protective hold. His lips brushed her temple. Bryn raised his eyebrows at the sight. He was probably wondering what he had just stumbled upon.

"Ellery, this is Bryn. My best friend, and the youngest commander in the king's guard. Bryn, this is Ellery." If Bryn was waiting for more than a first name, he wasn't going to get it clearly because Alexei was introducing her like a pop star, one name only.

The two nodded at each other politely.

Niceties out of the way, Alexei said, "How and why?"

"Aines sent a pigeon back, and Carwyn told them to turn back around. He said they were at the cabin. When he said he thought she may be *different*, I assumed where you were taking her since you clearly weren't heading home. I went to the cabin and tracked you down from there."

"And the why?"

"Aines wrote that you were most likely spellbound and had a suspicion where you were headed next. He is certainly more intuitive than I gave him credit for. I'm relieved that he's not all brawn and no brains. There is a little bit of a brain rattling around in there."

That is too vague of an answer, Ellery thought.

Then she saw Bryn give Alexei a look that said he would explain more later. She was sure he didn't want to say it in front of her. Alexei nodded in understanding. Damn them both! She had a right to know.

"I gather that there is more to be said but obviously either neither one of you want to hurt the poor woman's sensibilities or you are purposefully hiding it. The fact that you, a commander, are here can't be for a casual visit." Then she leveled a look at him. "Go ahead, I can take it."

Bryn laughed and met her gaze with an approving glance. "Not much for small talk, are you?"

"It's never been a skill that I was particularly good at."

He grinned. "For the record, it was because I didn't want to upset you, not because I'm hiding anything. You have a right to know. I am here to bring you both home, the spellbound and the binder herself."

"I'm not spellbound," Alexei scoffed like the notion was completely ridiculous. But was it, she wondered. Was she capable of something like that?

"While I'm pretty sure that is exactly what you would say if you were, I believe you. Even if you were, there are worse ways for a man to go than by following a beautiful woman around the last few days before his tragic demise."

"So, to summarize, to some I am some sort of savior here to avenge a kingdom, and to others I am nothing more than a wicked temptress leading handsome young men to their doom."

"Oh, you think we are handsome, do you?" Bryn said and waggled his eyebrows at her.

"Let's act for one second like you don't know you are." Then she looked at Alexei. "You know I didn't spellbind you."

"I know."

At the same time Bryn said, "That doesn't mean you aren't a temptress."

"Oh true, I am just out here collecting men like this?" She pointed down at herself. She hadn't bathed since the morning before when they left the cabin. She was rumpled and still smelled like campfire smoke.

"If he isn't spellbound, then you are just a terrible influence on my prince here. The same man that always toed the line is out on the lam with Westrim's most wanted."

She wanted to bite back a reply but she couldn't. *Truer words*, she thought, and blew out a breath. "It's not like I meant for it to happen like this."

"Why not? I have been trying to have that kind of influence on him for years. I'm impressed. I would say I wonder what you have that I don't, but…" Then he gave her a once over and grinned again. "Can't say I blame him. This takes the term sleeping with the enemy to a whole other level."

"Bryn, what the hell?" Alexei said, half outraged and half amused.

"What?" he said innocently. "I meant literally not figuratively. Unless there's something else that you want to tell me."

"There isn't."

"That's a shame." Then he looked back at her and winked. "I'm available, temptress."

"And I'm overjoyed," she said sarcastically and highly considered giving him the finger.

"And she's not the enemy," Alexei said.

"I have eyes and a brain. I can see what she is to you."

He ignored the comment. "How is Carwyn?"

"Oh, you know him. He's just a barrel of laughs as usual."

Alexei leveled him with a look, but Ellery could see the corner of his mouth tick up.

"You obviously got your fun quota from him," Bryn said.

Alexei looked at her. "He's not as stodgy as Bryn is making him out to be. He is…"

"A wet mop," Bryn finished his sentence.

"Come on, you love him as much as I do."

"Of course I do. Not only is he my king, he is the big brother I never had. But that doesn't change the fact that he is a crashing bore sometimes."

Ellery couldn't help but smile at the banter between them. She envied that. It was something she didn't have a lot of with many people. She wasn't sure what it said about her that her most meaningful interactions outside of work when she was with Lily, were with Clara, the neighbor she saw once a week as they crossed paths in the hall. When that was the person who was most likely to be your emergency contact, she had to consider that she was slightly unsocial, and needed to become a bit more familiar with some people.

"Honestly, how is he?"

"Worried sick. He tried to come himself, but I told him it was a bad idea. If it was dangerous, he needed to be home, so I offered."

Carwyn had always been overprotective. "I'm relieved he doesn't have half the army out looking for me."

"Trust me he thought about it, but he knew that it was important to go about everything as usual and not get everyone worked up. Besides, if she does somehow get to safety and do what she was meant to do, we will need the army back home defending the kingdom." Alexei didn't even want to think about that, so he pushed it to the back of his mind. He was worried about her, and only her, despite the fact that there was a very real chance that her safety might mean his downfall.

"I guess there's no point in bringing up why this has disaster written all over it."

Alexei shook his head letting him know it didn't matter. "Head home and say you didn't find me."

"Like they'll believe that."

Ellery almost laughed at the cocky statement, but something told her that it was the truth.

"I'm in it for the long haul. We'll figure it out together. We always have. I still can't believe Aines is out here on his high horse. He's been waiting a long time to try and hold something over you."

"He will have to get the hell in line, and it will be my pleasure to take care of him when the time is right. In the meantime, there is something else."

"There always is."

"What do you know about the brand?"

Bryn looked between the two, and his face showed just as much confusion as theirs when she outstretched her palm for him to look.

"You didn't know, either?"

They told him about the brands on the others from the night before. They had confirmed it was on those with magic in the blood.

"I knew that there was a way to do it, but never knew more than that. It must be above my pay grade."

"Mine too, apparently."

How was that even possible? she wondered.

"How did it happen?" Bryn asked and she explained the sword.

"It must have been enchanted," Bryn said absently, deep in thought.

"Do you think they knew that? That it was enchanted."

"There is no way to know for sure, but I would venture to guess that they do. It is more than a bit irritating that Aines has information we don't."

"We always knew that there were those tasked with looking for magic, but hearing about the prophesy fills in some blanks. I wonder who all knows about it."

She asked a question out loud that she had been wondering. Ever since Clara had spoken to them around the campfire, she'd needed to know more. "Why do you think it all happened in the first place? What made one side or the other so unhappy that it turned into this?"

"Not sure," Bryn said. "We don't know if something terrible happened or if their emotions took over. Surely they felt fear and jealousy, greed and desire where magic was concerned."

"That seems to be giving those emotions too much credit," Ellery said thoughtfully.

"Really, I don't think people give them enough. Certain emotions are extremely powerful."

"More powerful than magic?"

"I think they can push people into doing things they would never do otherwise, make decisions that they wouldn't normally make. I think that itself is a type of power, just maybe not always the good kind."

"If that is true than you are putting the blame on Westrim, when maybe Mearan did something to incite that fear."

"True," Bryn agreed. "There are two sides to every story, and I know that, and things are never normally black and white."

"I wish I knew more," Alexei said.

"You were young," Ellery countered.

"I was and suffocating with grief. I guess I let myself be sheltered and by the time I pulled myself out of missing my parents, it didn't relate to my everyday life."

"All we know is that someone or something is destined to open it again," Bryn said, and both sets of eyes met hers.

"It's my fault that they found her in the first place," Alexei said, his expression somber.

"Alexei, don't say that."

"The soldiers wouldn't have been out there at all if I hadn't been so hellbent on seeking one last hoorah before returning to my duty as soon-to-be king. Aines wouldn't have found you if I could have just kept walking that day you came here and let you go. I led them to you." His words struck Ellery for a moment. He didn't take her with him just to help her, but because he wanted her with him. He needed her in the same way that she had needed him.

"Okay, say it wasn't you. Say it was someone else. Maybe the next person wouldn't have been so understanding of the weird stranger I was, landing the way I did in this place. Maybe they would have seen me as a threat, or who knows what. Maybe I wouldn't be here right now. You saved me."

He was the one that had been unlucky when he found her, not the other way around. Seeing Bryn had reaffirmed for her what Alexei was risking by protecting her. Seeing part of his life firsthand gave her just a small piece of the whole. Feelings that she had suppressed from the first moment she laid eyes on him flooded through her. There was an awareness that lingered any time they came into the briefest of contact or locked eyes.

Alexei must have sensed her because he looked over, and his gaze held her own. She needed to break the silence and the pressure and emotions that were building inside of her. Though these were things that she would rather not deal with.

She wouldn't be the reason he was hurt. She knew that he would protect her. She trusted him to do the right thing. But at what cost? She had to find a way to leave him, to ensure his safety.

"I can make this much easier on everyone and head out tonight. You both can head home, and if you give me the map, I can find my way there. You won't be accused of treason, and I will be gone before they have time to send anyone else." Ellery's voice was strong and somber.

Alexei stared over at her. He spoke to Bryn with lethal calm but never took his eyes off of her. "Can you give us a minute?"

"I brought provisions." Bryn held up a bag. "Since we know Aines and company are further ahead I'll make a fire and we can eat. How about over there a bit further inside the woods?"

Alexei nodded, eyes still staring into hers, and it looked like there was anger lurking there.

She raised her hands up and pressed her fingertips into her temples. "I know you heard what he said. Neither one of you is safe. You won't be until I am gone. What if they get to us and realize that you aren't spellbound, but out here rambling around and actively committing treason of your own free will?"

He reached up and cupped the back of her neck and kept her eyes steady on his. "You aren't leaving me."

"I have been nothing but trouble from the moment that we met." She pulled away from his hand and backed away from him.

"I would find you." He followed her slowly, his voice still eerily calm, despite the emotions she could tell he had inside of him. She could practically feel them in her own body, and it made her chest ache.

She tipped her chin up in a look of defiance but before she could lash out, he reached for her and pulled her tight, his arms closing around her in an almost painful grip. "Don't leave me, Ellery. Not like that."

"What if I am what they say I am?" she asked as he held her head to his chest, and the fact that it felt so right made everything else feel so much worse. "It would change everything."

"What if it is you? What if you do change everything? That doesn't mean that change has to be bad. You are good, all of you. Nothing bad could possibly come from you."

"That isn't true."

"It is," he said instantly.

"How do you expect me to keep going on like nothing has happened? I'm a ticking time bomb that is going to go off and take you with me."

There was silence for a moment before she looked up at him. In the back of her mind, she kept hearing Aines say the word treason over and over. She should have taken it more seriously then, but after seeing Clara, and now Bryn, everything felt more real.

"I care about you," Ellery said with feeling.

He held in a sigh. If she only knew that caring was only a fraction of what he felt for her. She would really run if she knew how he truly felt.

"I care about you enough to keep going and damn the consequences. Stay with me and let's finish what we started. If you leave now and I go back, I'll be useless to everyone anyway from worrying about you. And you won't make it to where you need to go without me, which would put both of us in an even worse situation," he said logically, trying to pull at her voice of reason. "If we stick with the original plan, we will both be fine. Safe and sound at home in the end."

"And when I am gone?"

He realized she feared for him, what they would do to him.

"I'll be fine, Ellery," he said in a bit of a mocking tone. "I'm going to be king, after all."

Her leaving would be a worse fate than anything else. What would he do without her smile, the strength in her eyes, and the softness of her body curled up next to him at night.

He knew without a doubt that she would haunt him long after she was gone. Long after she was home, and long after she had convinced herself that their time together had just been another dream.

Chapter Eighteen

Bryn sat beside the fire he had just coaxed to life. They were concealed by trees and the darkness of the night with only the light of the moon and the glow of the fire to push the gloom back. Ellery let her gaze drift between the treetops as she looked into the infinite night. The stars glittered in the sky, far away and out of reach. The fire crackled, and she sighed contentedly as its warmth surrounded her and provided a welcome reprieve from the cool breeze that filled the night air.

After they ate, she clasped her hands together on her lap and used the pad of her thumb to trace the outline of the brand on her palm. "I would like to clarify something with you two. Do a quick recap." They each nodded in turn. "So, either my kingdom, and I say that loosely because who knows, is plagued with a bunch of homicidal maniacs or yours was scared enough, greedy enough, to strip an entire kingdom of everything that they were without provocation. And now they believe that I am the one thing standing in the way of that peaceful reign they imagine?"

Bryn picked up a stick and stoked the fire again before looking at her. "I would say that is pretty accurate, which is why we need to make moves, and fast." Silence filled the air, and only the crack of the fire dared to make a noise. "What is your master plan here, Alex?"

"It's not much of a plan. At first, I was just planning to head to the cottage and sort things out from there, but the other day after Aines showed up, I knew that I had to bump up the timeline."

"Of course it would have to be Aines out here on a power trip," Bryn muttered.

Alexei nodded and thought of the smirk that Aines often had on his face and the unsettling glint in his eye. He rarely smiled, but when he did it seemed almost cruel, like a cat playing with its prey before killing it. The thought that Aines was currently seeking Ellery as his prey made Alexei seethe.

"He's a good soldier, I'll give him that, but there is something else going on there. He is too unpredictable. Not to mention, he seriously wants to have a go at you," Bryn stated.

"I would be more than happy to oblige anytime he wants to settle it."

The thought made Ellery shudder. She didn't want him anywhere near Aines. "He looks at you like he hates you."

"He does," he said, and it almost seemed nonchalant. "I couldn't tell you why exactly, and I'm not sure that he could either. Anyway," he said and looked back to Bryn, wanting to change the subject and take the worry out of Ellery's eyes. "When they left, I knew any other choice had been taken away, and that I had to take her there. That is her best chance at getting home."

"Which is where?" Bryn asked. His eyes darted between Ellery and Alexei. "Where exactly is home?" Bryn said to clarify.

Alexei paused for a minute. Even though besides his uncle, Bryn was the only person he would trust with his own life, he realized it was harder to trust when it was Ellery's life on the line.

"Far away from here," Alexei answered before Ellery could.

"One of the smaller regions?"

Alexei shook his head no, not wanting to give anything more away.

"Any place I may have heard of?" Bryn stretched his legs and crossed them at the ankle, giving off the impression that he was relaxed. She saw through that and knew what he was asking. She understood the importance of it.

"Not likely." Then Alexei shot Bryn a look that told him that line of questioning was over.

"I've been wondering," Ellery said, taking the break in conversation to ask a question she had been turning over in her head. "Why would they think I, well, Mearan, would want to spellbind Alexei in the first place?" she asked Bryn.

"If you are in fact the key to breaking their curse, they will soon be restored back to their full power. Upon that restoration if Mearan has the future king of Westrim, their rival kingdom, in their grasp as well, it is more than a power play." His eyes were serious. "It is checkmate."

She nodded because it made sense. How could she fight that thought process?

"I don't want you to worry about that," Alexei said to Ellery, then he looked back at Bryn. "I figure we will make it there by tomorrow evening. After we make sure Ellery is safe, we will backtrack and sort things out at home. If what Clara said was true, if she is the key, and she does what she is meant to do, they will send her back home if that is her wish. We will deal with the rest of the aftermath when she is gone. For now, let's go to bed and deal with the rest in the morning."

Alexei's words rang out with the authority of a leader, making it clear that the conversation was over. They all needed rest.

"Why don't I take the first watch?" Bryn offered.

As they did the other night, they put the packs together by the fire. Although they wouldn't need the body heat with the fire, neither said anything and set up together. She lay down. This time he lay down behind her and she felt him press along her back. The warmth of him enveloped her as the weight of his arms went around her.

"Is this okay?" he asked and she nodded.

She let out a contented sigh, and he pulled her back tighter against him. They had slept beside each other the other night, but this felt different. A newer intimacy between them made her heart ache with desires still tucked away in her. The depth of her feelings for him seemed to be their own bit of magic, and she had the fleeting thought that she wished she could use magic to make sure they could be together in any world.

"Some part of me is still considering the fact that this could all be a dream, just a much longer one," she said softly.

"Would that be a bad thing?" he asked. She turned around in the circle of his arms. He followed the movement and rolled onto his back. She looked into his eyes before resting her head on his shoulder. Surprise flickered in their gray depths when she nodded.

"I never thought I would know you, or this place, as I know you now. I always thought that you would live on in my dreams." She paused like she was going to hold something back but didn't. "I'm afraid that I'll wake up to realize that you were never real after all." She whispered the next part as she traced circles along the rough fabric that covered his muscled chest. "I think it would break my heart."

He reached up and covered her hand with his own. "I don't know everything that is going on, and I have next to no answers right now to solve that, but I can tell you this," he looked down at their clasped hands. "This is the one thing that I know is real."

He felt her relax at that, and when she settled more comfortably against him thoughts of her washed over him. Alexei wasn't sure if he had fallen in love with her the moment he saw her, or if it was in the dozens of memories he had stored up over the last few days. Everything about them had been quick and intense. It was no wonder that the spark he had felt for her caught fire. A flame that consumed him. It was the kind of love that stories were made of, where the prince met his true love, and they lived happily ever after. Too bad their ending wouldn't have the "ever after" part, he thought gravely.

Even though the world around her felt just as tangible as it had before she had fallen asleep, she knew she was dreaming from the way she was looking down at herself curled against Alexei. It could have been some sort of out of body experience, but she had had enough dreams over the last few months to recognize the way they felt.

She watched the couple lie there for a moment and was surprised at the feeling that swept through her. She had never wanted to need someone or to depend on them. But with him it was easy. She waited for that feeling where she felt vulnerable. Whenever she would feel trapped, she'd run, but she didn't feel that way. She liked the way she felt about him. She needed him. It brought equal amounts pleasure and pain knowing that even though she felt that way, her time with him was limited.

"I knew you were into blondes."

Ellery practically jumped out of her skin when she heard the familiar voice behind her.

CHAPTER NINETEEN

Ellery spun around and there was Lily. She was sitting on a log by the fire. Ellery didn't know whether to laugh or cry. Seeing a familiar face felt so good. The dancing flames of the fire illuminated Lily's delicate features and showed off the mischief in her eyes. Shock and relief thrummed through Ellery as she latched onto the knowledge that Lily, her coworker and friend, was there.

"What are you doing here?" Ellery asked as she ran over and simultaneously sat and threw her arms around Lily in one fell swoop. Delight raced through Ellery at having another piece of familiarity, of home. She hadn't realized that she would miss much of anything from her world. She tended to keep herself so closed off, a hazard of moving around so much in foster care, she guessed. But to look at her friend, the way she smiled, the way her dimple winked out at her when she did, the calming comfort she brought and the joy, Ellery realized there was more happiness in her life than she'd previously thought.

"You don't seem too surprised," Lily said after Ellery released her. Lily pulled back and looked her up and down.

"Trust me, I wish I was."

Lily took in Ellery's rough and ready clothing, her uncombed hair, and unmanicured nails. She let out a whistle, a habit she had when she was thinking. "Rough time since you got here?" Lily asked casually, eyebrow raised. Ellery was too excited to see Lily to tease back. Lily had asked as casually as she would have asked about how her work shift went. It seemed like a lifetime had passed since then.

"Why didn't you tell me?" Ellery said, searching Lily's caramel eyes.

"About what? The fact that I am magic… the fact that you are? That I belonged to another world? That…" She cut herself off and shook her head. "There is only so much that I can say. I can say this, I wasn't sure if starting off our friendship by telling you that I was from another world would have been the best move on my part."

Ellery understood where she was coming from. Hearing Lily ask the questions aloud made Ellery realize she would have just written Lily off as losing her mind. Obviously, Lily needed to be close to Ellery the way Mrs. Hansen had been, so Lily couldn't just blurt everything out.

But where Mrs. Hansen's heart and motives had seemed straightforward, Lily's weren't so clear. At least, not yet. Was Lily just using her for something?

"I thought we were friends. This is a big secret to keep for so long, Lily." That was what was bothering her, she realized. She thought they had been fairly close friends, and she couldn't deny the feeling of betrayal that consumed her.

This time Lily looked at her. "We are friends."

Hearing that took a bit of the sting out.

"I wish I could tell you more, but just know that I was there to help you. I still am." Then she smiled again. "As your friend."

"Were you there with Mrs. Hansen?" Ellery asked but then shook her head. "Clara, I mean, back home?"

"I was not," Lily answered rather quickly.

"But you know her?"

She nodded but clearly wasn't going to give any more details on the subject. Ellery briefly wondered if she couldn't, or if she didn't want to.

"I do," Lily said, meeting Ellery's gaze.

"What can you tell me?"

"Not a lot. I'm sure Clara told you what she could," she said but her eyes narrowed ever so slightly, making the statement feel like it meant so much more. It almost sounded like it was a question, an inquiry, instead of a statement. Everything was so cryptic.

"Are you from Mearan?"

"I'm like Clara. I can cross barriers, but unlike her I can't take anyone with me. I came the last couple of months to ensure that you ended up exactly where you are right now."

Not a clear answer, but it was something. "You kept an eye on me?" Ellery said, her heart wanting to feel like Lily was an ally in all this.

"So to speak, yes."

"Let me get this straight. You are from this world, but you came to my world, and now you are back? Not only back in this world, but somehow also in my dream?" She'd had to choke down a lot of information that last few days, and this was even confusing for her.

"Like I said, I cross barriers. You know how Clara can take someone with her as part of her… gift? Well, I can cross the barriers of someone's mind as part of my gift."

Ellery knew there was a whole lot to unpack about that statement but didn't even know where to start. She was also surprised she got that amount of information out of her. It seemed like they were all pretty limited in what they could share, for some unknown irritating reason, which was in itself a huge concern.

"We will have plenty of time to talk about all of that later," Lily said briskly.

"So, you can't or you won't talk about it?"

"Maybe a little bit of both. What I can talk about is the fact that I am desperately going to miss having my food delivered and my kindle. Oh, how I am going to miss instant access to books. This world needs to be spiced up a bit. Not that I think the internet is going to be a part of it anytime soon, but a few changes here and there couldn't hurt."

"Lily, focus. If that is even your name." Ellery looked at her accusingly, trying not to get sidetracked.

Lily looked back and there was a bit of hurt in her gaze. "It is my name, and the time that we shared together was real. I'm sorry for the rest of it, but I couldn't tell you. Just know who I was when I was with you was me."

Ellery nodded. "Okay, but why are you here then if you can't tell me anything?"

"You need to take another look at the map," Lily said. She stood and walked toward the couple now lying at her feet.

"Why?"

"Why does anyone use a map?"

"For directions."

"Exactly."

Ellery should have tried to get more out of her about directions, but her next question came out completely different. "What can you tell me about Alexei?"

Lily looked down at him and then back at her with a grin. "I can tell you that I wasn't wrong about the four percent body fat."

Ellery remembered the day Lily had told that story, and Ellery had thought she was going out of her mind. Then Ellery thought of the night before, crawling into his lap and being pressed against his warm body. Her cheeks flushed.

"That I can see for myself."

"And feel," Lily said out of the corner of her mouth. Ellery chose to ignore her.

"Can you tell me if he is somehow being forced, by fate or something or someone else to help me? I don't want him to get hurt because of me."

Lily seemed to think about it for a minute. "Whatever decision he is making is because it is something he wants to do, wants to risk."

"What will happen if I don't make it to Mearan?"

They heard a voice. It was as if it started narrating the dream and boomed down into it. She realized it was Alexei yelling her name. He sounded panicked, scared. Was he trying to wake her up?

"The map will guide you, and you will have to take it from there on your own."

"And if I do make it, what then?"

Lily went to answer, and Ellery felt them both fading away.

"No no no no no no no," she chanted and woke up.

~ ~ ~

Alexei woke up and instantly knew something was off. Ellery was still curled against him but even against his warmth and the fire, she was cold. Ice cold. He checked for her pulse and was relieved when he felt it beating strongly. She was still breathing, but she was so pale and so cold. He sat up and hauled her against him to try and warm her. Her hands dropped limply at her sides.

"Ellery, wake up."

Nothing, although he thought he saw her eyes flicker at his voice.

"Ellery," he said again, almost pleading. Still nothing.

"Please, Ellery." He had a feeling that he could yell himself hoarse and it wouldn't make a difference, but that didn't stop him from trying. He was about to take her to Bryn when her eyes opened. The piercing relief that tore through him made him shudder. Ellery's eyes looked confused as she looked up at him under her thick dark lashes.

"What happened?" She looked around and the baffled look on her face terrified and relieved him at the same time.

He pulled her close and held on tightly. Something had clearly happened, but she waited a few minutes before she asked again. Reluctantly he pulled back to look down at her, wanting to see that she had color back in her face that had gone so incredibly pale as she slept.

"Magic," he breathed, and this time when he said it, she didn't object. How else could Lily have crossed her mind and waltzed into her dreams? "Something took you… somehow, and you were so cold, so pale."

As much as she wanted to turn away from all of it, magic existed, and she was wrapped up in the core of it.

"I was okay, am okay, I promise." She stood up to stretch and told him what happened. As she did, they both seemed to relax. Alexei moved to hold her tightly again, like he couldn't help it and needed to feel her there. She suddenly became too aware of how her body felt against his. She should have backed away. Instead, she leaned up, never taking her eyes off of his, and gave them both a moment to make up their mind.

The world around them stood still and everything else faded away. All she saw, all she felt, was him. She finally did what she had thought of doing since dreams of him plagued her and left her feeling restless with need. In a slow, delicious motion, she pressed her lips to his. They were soft against hers, but she felt how he had gone very still. After a moment she leaned back.

"That was too much?" she said quickly when his face was unreadable, embarrassed that she thought he had felt the same.

Her lips had brushed his, slow and gentle. That sweet, soft kiss ruined him.

"Not at all," he breathed out right before he crushed his mouth to hers.

She opened her lips to him and let out a small groan when he swept his tongue inside. Something loosened in him with the feel and taste of her completely surrounding him, a hunger that couldn't be sated. He had wanted to do that since the moment he saw her. How had he held back for so long? Had he known he wanted her that much?

Ellery felt the force behind the kiss, a need that took her breath away. The demanding mouth on hers slowed and turned to smooth caresses. She had been kissed before, but never like that. He kissed her with surety, possessiveness, and a desire that thrummed through her. Feeling his need for her was exhilarating. Her body relaxed against him, eagerly and willingly surrendering to the feel of him. When he felt that surrender, he smoothly lifted her up in his strong arms, and she wrapped her legs around him.

He walked them back a few feet until her back was up against a tree, his mouth never leaving hers. He knew that he should slow down but her body urged him on, and he wanted to touch her, taste her, be with her. He felt her melt into him as her hands moved to his hair, holding on. He raised one of his own hands to her cheek before he slid it back into the endless sea of brown hair as his body anchored hers. He wasn't sure where one kiss ended and the next began. When he felt that he soon wouldn't be able to stop himself from going further, he broke the kiss.

Alexei saw the heat in her eyes, the desire, and knew that they could have done what they both wanted to right there, but the few rational brain cells that were still in working order reminded him that this shouldn't be their first time together, so he would wait. He leaned down to kiss her softly before giving her bottom lip a little nip. He wrapped one arm around her back and felt the brush of the bark against his skin, before trailing a soothing hand up and down her back that had no doubt rubbed against the bark. He realized he had been rough with her, rougher than he should have. Still, he held her against the tree, her legs still tightly wrapped around him, and her body pressed against his. Neither one moved to let the other go.

"I'm…"

"Don't you dare say sorry," she said, trying to keep her voice steady, somehow reading his mind.

"I shouldn't have been so rough with you." Something had been let loose inside of him at the thought of something happening to her.

"You weren't."

He nodded but didn't meet her eyes as he gently, reluctantly, lowered her feet to the ground. She could tell he had a lot more on his mind.

"Something could have happened to you while you were stuck in that dream, and I wouldn't have known."

"I'm fine. I'm right here."

"But you weren't. Physically maybe, but not really here. You were so cold."

"Please don't feel like you have to protect me, Alexei. It's not your responsibility. You have done enough." She had been taking care of herself for years, and he had enough responsibilities and people to worry about. He didn't need the weight of one more on his shoulders.

"Do you think that is all it is? That I just wanted to protect you out of a sense of responsibility?"

She wanted to say that his whole life was out of responsibility, but she didn't dare utter the words.

"That time between when I woke up and you opened your eyes felt like a lifetime." He leaned his forehead down to hers. "It's not out of responsibility, Ellery. Or not just. I would take care of anyone because that is just who I am. But you. I have wanted you from the moment I saw you, and every moment since. It is much more. More than responsibility, more than…"

He didn't get to finish as they heard Bryn's hushed voice calling their names. It cost him to pull away from her, but he leaned back and scorched her with a look that made her bones melt before he pressed one last quick kiss to her lips. He had never wanted anything more than to finish what they had started.

She tried to take a step away from him to put some distance between them, doing her best to beat back the desire pumping through her. Instead, Alexei pulled her closer and rubbed the pad of his thumb against her bottom lip. Despite the way his chest rose and fell as rapidly as hers did, he sounded incredibly put together when he spoke.

"Over here."

Bryn emerged from the thicket and smiled when his eyes landed on her and then on Alexei. "I swore I heard you screaming, but then I thought I was just dreaming. I couldn't go back to sleep, so I decided to see for myself that everything was fine. Everything okay here?"

She let out a shaky breath and nodded. She was fairly certain that her hair was mussed, and her lips swollen, but she did her best to appear composed and focus on why he was worried in the first place. If he felt the tension, or the desire pumping off them in waves, he was all "mum's the word."

"What happened?" Bryn asked casually as he put his hands in the pockets of his trousers. He had certainly stumbled into the middle of something.

Ellery found her voice and steadied herself as she relayed what happened. It was like she was constantly narrating her own life. It was tedious but necessary.

"Why don't you two get some sleep. Tomorrow is going to come sooner than we think."

Alexei shook his head. "I can take this watch."

Bryn nodded to Ellery when she wasn't looking and raised his eyebrows as if giving his friend a clue. "How about we switch off in a bit?"

Alexei slid his friend a grateful look. "See you soon," he said in answer, and when Bryn wandered off, they stood there in silence together. He let her take the lead.

"What am I?" she said tentatively and looked down at herself and then to him with uncertainty pouring out of her. She was thinking of everything that had happened, and how she was at the center of all of it.

Alexei wasn't sure of magic, the good and the bad of it, but he was sure about her. "Whatever is inside of you is perfect." He said it so simply, so honestly, that it soothed something inside of her that threatened to suffocate her. "Soon we will have all the answers."

She thought about their destination, and another thought crossed her mind. "What direction will we be heading tomorrow?"

"East," he said and motioned to the direction they would take.

It was the complete opposite direction of where she had been heading earlier, and something in her, instinct maybe, told her that there was a reason she had been drawn in that direction.

"Can I see the map again?"

"Sure." He went to his pack and got it. The fire was still burning, and they were able to look at it in the light it provided.

As soon as she saw it, she knew it wasn't right. Something went through her, and she shivered as if it tickled along her senses, as if some forgotten memory was trying to make its way out of her consciousness and into reality. "We are heading in the wrong direction."

"How do you know that?"

"Think of what I told you Lily said, about the directions."

Alexei nodded but looked back at the map and she could tell he didn't believe her.

"You don't believe me?" she asked as evenly as possible, trying to keep the edge out of her voice.

He continued to look at the map, not meeting her eyes. "Of course I believe what you told me, all of it, but how does that change what a map says? Maybe she meant something else. Why don't you get some sleep, and we'll talk about it in the morning?"

"Don't placate me. I don't need sleep. I need you to listen to me," she said and slapped her hand down on the middle of the map in anger so he would be forced to look at her. When he didn't, she pulled her hand back. Before she could say anything, she was surprised to see Alexei looking at her transfixed.

"What?" she said, trying to keep the bite of irritation out of her voice.

"Do that again," he said, but couldn't meet her eyes. He kept them on the map.

She huffed out a breath. "Throw a temper tantrum?"

At that he smirked slightly and looked up into her eyes and grinned. "No, sweetheart. Put your hand on the map again."

She gave him an odd look, but shrugged and laid her hand flat on the map. Their eyes went wide as it shimmered and ink started to flow, before it disappeared altogether.

CHAPTER TWENTY

She should have snatched her hand back, but fear had her holding still. Good thing she did because in another moment the words and pictures started seeping back into the map. Slowly she pulled her hand away, and she could have sworn her skin hummed, leaving a slight tingle behind. She saw with shock that the map had rearranged itself, that where she had been heading would lead them right to where they needed to be.

"That's impossible," she breathed as she turned her hand over, as if looking at it for the first time. Even though she had very literally performed magic, it seemed too unreal.

He paced around for a minute before another idea struck him. He didn't want to push her, but he wanted to test a theory. "Let's try with the compass."

She followed his train of thought and nodded. He handed the compass to her and took a step back.

The compass started to shake slightly in her hand. She could feel it vibrate against her skin, but instead of the direction she had been walking in, the needle pointed directly towards him. She was sure it was a sign, an indication of some sort, but she wasn't sure of what.

She stepped forward, closer to him as if guided by some mysterious force and then slowly walked back and around him in a wide circle before zig zagging around a bit. Wherever she walked the needle found its way to him.

After a minute she whispered, "You need to see this."

He walked closer and she pointed at the needle, indicating for him to watch it. Even as he looked down, she told him to walk around her. As he did, the needle followed his path always stopping firmly and unequivocally on him.

"What does it mean?" she asked in wonder.

Was he the direction that she was supposed to take? She remembered how she felt the day she met him, that she needed him for whatever came next. She thought back to that, and wondered if that was the only reason they felt the way that they did for each other, like they were connected by something more powerful than either of them could comprehend.

She had felt compelled to be near him, even in dreams. Deep down, she knew now that it wasn't just a coincidence that they had met. Fate had brought them together for some unknown purpose. Was that why she wanted him so badly? It didn't make logical sense how much she wanted him, so quickly, so completely. Was it all because it was fated from the beginning? She wanted to express it to him but held back.

"Another question we don't have the answer to," he muttered and rubbed the top half of his face with his hand.

Although they couldn't explain each part of who she was or why she was here, she knew one thing for certain. They were supposed to be together.

The next morning Ellery and Alexei worked together as they cleaned up camp. The smoky smell of her hair kept drifting to her nose and threatened to push through the headache that was trying to move in. She remembered how long she had to rest the last time she had a migraine there. They couldn't afford another setback like that again.

"This smell is going to give me a headache. I'm going to go wash it off in the stream. Why don't you go get Bryn, and we can meet back here for breakfast and then head out?"

They had switched posts in the middle of the night but switched back closer to dawn when Bryn was too restless to sleep, and Alexei was too restless to be that far from Ellery. He was reluctant to let her out of his sight but nodded when he remembered that Aines and the others were not only ahead of them but heading in the wrong direction.

Maybe it wasn't the right time, but he had stopped himself a dozen times that morning from telling her the thoughts that had crossed his mind and taken hold in the middle of the night. He was going to lay it all out there and give her something to think about. She couldn't stay. It wasn't safe, but he could go with her. He had turned the thought over and over in his head and found that it felt exactly right.

The only thing he wanted more than the kingdom was her. There was a small voice in him saying how selfish leaving his people, leaving Carwyn, was. Maybe his uncle didn't want to rule. But he overrode those thoughts. Carwyn had taken a lot on but had flourished over the years and had fallen in love with what he did as interim king. He would write to Carwyn and have Bryn take the note back to him. Alexei loved the people and knew they would be taken care of by his uncle.

He would need to ensure his kingdom's safety. If Ellery could somehow release the magic back to Mearan, it could be dangerous, but he believed that under the circumstances she would be able to ask the leaders of Mearan for almost anything and could then guarantee their safety.

"What do you think we are going to find when we get there today?" she asked and interrupted his train of thought.

"To be honest, I don't know."

She reached for his hand, and he held on tight. "I'm scared," she said so softly it crushed him. Especially knowing how hard it would be for her to admit that to him, let alone to herself.

"This is going to work. We will make it to Mearan, and they will set everything straight. You'll be home safe and sound soon enough."

She nodded. "I think it is going to work, too, but that's why I am so scared."

"What if I went with you?" he asked.

She pulled back and he took in the look of her, the shock on her pretty face.

"Why would you even joke about that?" she admonished him.

He grabbed her hand when she tried to step back. "What if I went with you?" he repeated.

"But you are… you can't…" She looked bewildered as she sputtered it out, but he didn't miss the quick flash of desire in her eyes. That spurred him on.

"Carwyn is one of the best rulers our kingdom has ever seen. My people would be safe and continue to thrive under his leadership. You aren't safe here, so let's go. Together." He wanted to be with her, in whatever world they ended up in. He knew how outrageous it all sounded, but he wanted it anyway. Wanted her. Despite the fact that it made no sense, he knew they could make it work. He could picture it. If they ever found a way, maybe they would come back together one day, when things settled down, but if not, then that was okay too.

"What about when you get sick of me one day, and realize that you followed me, gave up everything, everyone, because fate somehow forced your hand?" He went to reply, but she shook her head to stop him. "There is a reason that you were the one to find me," she said, thinking back to the compass. "You are the one who has spoken of fate. What if that's what it is, the reason why we feel what we feel? Because some unseen guiding force is making us feel that way for each other. You'll resent it one day and resent me when you think of everything that you left behind."

She believed that he had no idea what he was truly offering because he was so tangled up in desire and adventure. As much as she wanted it, she wouldn't take his choices away from him. Instead of answering he kissed her gently when she expected it fast and hard. He trailed lazy kisses down her face before he grazed his lips along her chin and followed the path to where her pulse had quickened. He laid a long, soft kiss there as if he could soothe it. When he finally lifted his lips to hers again, she turned her head and tried her best to keep her mind clear and focus her thoughts.

"You'll hate me for it one day," she insisted.

A tear formed at the corner of her eye, and he leaned down to kiss it away. He tasted the salt from her tear as it absorbed into his skin. "I couldn't hate you. Not when everything about you makes me happier than I have ever been in my life. Tell me you don't feel the same way," he said and challenged her.

"But how do you know if that is you, or if that is fate making you feel that way?" she said and saw the frustration building in him.

"You can't tell me that what I have inside for you is because of something intertwined with fate. What I feel for you, what is in me, wants everything that is in you. Everything that you are, everything that you will be. That doesn't have anything to do with fate."

"Doesn't it?" she said, and his eyes flashed in warning.

He leaned down and when his lips were a breath away from her own, he spoke in a low, fierce whisper. "You don't belong to the fates." He brought his hand up to her cheek and held it steady when she went to pull away. "You belong to me." A kiss, this time quick and hard had feelings whipping through her that left her panting as if to prove a point. "Just like I belong to you. You feel it. I know you do."

She couldn't deny that. She wouldn't. "Wanting me isn't a good enough reason to give up everything."

"Loving you is."

The weight and the truth of those words soaked into her and crumbled whatever defenses she had.

"I never thought that I would feel this way about anyone. I certainly didn't think I would feel this way now, and with you, but maybe that's why it is right. Who cares if it doesn't make sense. Love isn't always clean cut. It is messy and complicated. So is what I feel for you, but can you look at me and tell me that you don't feel the same?"

She nodded her head as if to say yes, but the tears fell and before she knew it, she was shaking her head. He was right, she couldn't say she didn't feel the same.

"Maybe one day we will find a way to come back together. Maybe one day you and I will have the ability to go back and forth between both worlds." Alexei's voice was comforting. "Once the magic is released again, maybe anything is possible for us."

"And if not?" she asked.

He found it encouraging that she even asked and jumped on it.

"Then I will happily live in your world."

She tried to speak again, and he covered her mouth with his, stopping whatever thoughts were going to come next, hoping to kiss her until there were no more. When he broke the kiss, she was breathless as she looked up at him. He wanted to take her somewhere safe and kiss away every uncertain thought, every scared feeling. There would be time enough for that soon enough he reminded himself. His eyes seemed to grin down at her.

Before he could say anything else or kiss her again, she gave him a pointed look and raised two fingers to his lips.

"We aren't done talking about this."

He nodded but she knew he wasn't listening. He had already made up his mind regardless of the consequences.

~   ~   ~

Giddy excitement filled Ellery as she headed toward the stream. She somehow felt hot and cold at the same time, and tried to push away all of the reasons it couldn't work. She washed off quickly and was ready to get going because now she knew she was going to be starting the rest of her life. She knew in her heart it was going to work, that they would find the power to take her home, and he was giving her the incredible honor of going with her. She thought of him at her apartment, visiting her at the library. She thought of taking him to a museum, a baseball game. There were thousands of things that they would experience together. All of that and more was waiting for them.

She toweled off and got dressed. He had packed her another brown pair of breeches and a plain black t-shirt. She smiled as she wrung her hair out and thought of him eating a hot dog from a street vendor. She went still when she realized someone was there. She knew it and felt it more than she heard them. Slowly she turned around to look into a pair of ice blue eyes raking over her body.

"Don't mind me. I've just been enjoying the show," Aines said.

CHAPTER TWENTY-ONE

The hairs on the back of her neck stood up as soon as she heard that familiar voice. His words were low and lethal. They seemed to surround her like a vise, making it hard to breathe. She felt as though every inch of her skin was crawling and wanted nothing more than to run. She reminded herself she wasn't as powerless as she was the other day. There were a few tools at her disposal, so she kept her feet firmly in place and started to pack up her bag like he didn't matter. Something she was sure would infuriate him.

"How did you find me?" She couldn't stop herself from asking, despite trying to sound nonchalant.

He gave her a self-satisfied smirk and closed the small distance between them. She turned like she was going to run, and he grabbed her roughly. He pulled her back against him. The hands were a lot rougher with her this time and the gesture cruel. Despite that, it was exactly what she hoped he would do. All she had to do was bide her time for the right moment.

She was revolted, but more than getting away, she had to keep her secret safe. Because of this, she had her fingers folded in so tightly she could feel the tips of her nails cutting into her palm. He somehow already knew because he went right for her hand. She resisted.

"Don't hide it from me, love." He said it soft and soothing like a lover, while he kept the one wrist in his hand, so tightly it hurt. He used the other to pry the fingers away. All the while he kept her in the circle of his arms. His eyes lit up at seeing the brand, and he used his fingertips to trace it.

"You see, when this brand is on someone, it marks you, but it is also its own form of tracker, made possible by…"

"Magic," she whispered and finished his sentence. It didn't make any sense that his kingdom had that kind of power. They were the ones that fought so vehemently against it. Were they somehow magical too?

"Exactly. Aren't you a quick study. That answers some lingering questions as to whether or not Alexei was simply using you for extracurricular activities."

She stayed silent. She didn't even like Alexei's name on his lips.

"There are some of us tasked with this, who can feel and hear the brand. You are the first one I have ever been able to try this out on. I could feel you the closer that you got. Yesterday we thought we had lost your trail completely until you touched the sword. I left it behind in the hopes that you were near, it was a long shot, but it paid off handsomely," he sneered at her, gloating. "Who knows if we would have found you in enough time otherwise. What a clever girl you were for finding it. How did you know I left it behind just for you?"

She paled when she realized she had essentially caught herself, that the sword had somehow truly been enchanted.

"Yes, sweetheart," he crooned. "We had been planning the best way to separate you from the others, but lucky for me, you made it too easy on me when you left without Alexei this morning. You should have stayed with him, you know. All he wanted to do was keep you safe, and he would have. For once he isn't going to get what he wants."

There was a hardness in his eyes when he spoke of Alexei. It was bone-chilling, and she wondered what made him hate him so bad, jealousy maybe, or something else, she wondered if he even knew.

The anger in Aines at the thought of Alexei made his hands tighten on her upper arms to the point of pain, but that was okay. She needed him that close. While his mind was somewhere else, she planted her feet and thrust her hips back. Just as Alexei said, it caught him off balance, and she felt him lean over her. In the next moment that was no more than a blur, she side-stepped and turned around, made a fist the way that he had showed her. With vehemence she punched him right in the groin. She felt the impact and saw the way he crumpled.

She didn't have any time for a victory dance and turned to run, thinking if she could make it back to the camp that Alexei would be back. Everything would be fine. She turned back to look at Aines once and saw that he was still kneeling on the ground. She knew it wouldn't be for long. Before she turned her head back around, she ran into something solid. Unfortunately for Ellery, it was a human, and not a friendly one.

She didn't have any time to think who had grabbed her because he turned her away and shoved something against her face. He held it against her nose and mouth. It was a rag she realized, doused in something. She tried to fight and desperately wanted to breathe in clean air. She scratched at the hand that so tightly held the rag that was soaked in chemicals and leaking fumes against her mouth. She tried to pull away but the more she struggled the quicker her breaths came and went, sucking the nasty stuff into her lungs. The more it flowed through her body the less control she had over herself. Her arms felt heavy and lost their strength. They fell to her sides as she lost control fully, and her legs followed suit.

She thought of Alexei as the darkness closed in on her.

~ ~ ~

Alexei walked back toward camp and before he went to get Bryn, looked down at their makeshift bed from the night before. The sight of it made him smile. He leaned down to fold up the blanket when something connected with the back of his head. He groaned in pain as the impact jarred through his body, a sharp ringing filling his ears. He stumbled forward and felt his eyelids grow heavy. His vision blurred before he was engulfed in darkness.

He slowly opened his eyes, and the light from the sun made him flinch. He felt a sharp pain in his head as he tried to sit up and realized that he had been unconscious. A memory of what happened came flooding back into his mind. He was attacked from behind. He heard a noise coming from behind him and quickly turned to grab a rock by him, only to find the maker of that noise was Bryn. He dropped the rock and went to stand, taking in his surroundings for the first time.

Wordlessly, Bryn pointed to two soldiers, his soldiers, who had been apprehended and were tied to a sturdy tree, their wrists bound tightly with rope. The soldiers wore his emblem on their clothes, and cold rage settled on his chest.

"Are you okay?"

Alexei nodded and kept his eyes on the two soldiers tied up. He had trained with them often in the past and would barely recognize them for how they looked at him now with disdain.

"I have two more tied up about fifty yards from here. How many were there at the cottage that day?"

Alexei tried to think over the rage and the pounding in his head. "Six."

"Are you sure? How many fingers?" he asked and held his hand up.

Alexei swatted it away. "I'm sure."

"There are two left out there on the loose, then."

Alexei tried to quickly assess their situation and looked to Bryn. "Was Aines one of the ones that you tied up?"

He could tell from the deafening silence between them that he wasn't. He cursed under his breath. He knew there was something more to Aines, something edgy that never really sat right with him. But Aines had been too sly to ever truly give Alexei a reason to feel the way he was now. It made him uneasy to think what that man was capable of.

Alexei walked toward the soldiers and leaned close to Finn's face. His voice was low and guttural. His fear for Ellery was almost shadowed by the anger that whipped through him. "Where is she?"

Both men remained silent, but he saw a flicker in Finn's eyes at his tone. Bradan spoke up, probably worried the other soldiers held captive would cave. "We don't know," he said firmly, and held his gaze, his eyes never wavering. As if he thought that would save him, Finn nodded slightly in agreement.

"Should I tell you what I know?" Alexei barely recognized the voice speaking as his own with the cold menace that dripped from it. "That when we make it back home your life won't be worth a damn thing. That is," he paused for emphasis, "if I even allow you to keep it."

He saw fear flicker in Finn's eyes again and decided to zero in on him. "Now," he said calmly and pulled the knife out of his pocket, twirling it around in his fingers, "tell me what I want to know, unless you want to be food for the forest."

Bradan sneered. "You wouldn't dare."

Without hesitation he walked over and put the tip of the knife at the base of Finn's throat with the slightest pressure and locked eyes with Bradan. "That's where you are wrong. The only thing keeping me from pinning you to that tree with your sword is your knowledge of her whereabouts. If you can't help me with that, I'm afraid I have no more use for you."

Finn must have believed him because his brown eyes widened in terror. "Aines was going after her."

Bryn spoke next, sensing that Alexei was on the brink. "He might not have found her."

"He did," Bradan said, and Alexei could tell the man believed it. "He followed the," he stopped and seemed to try to find the right word for what he was going to convey, "the pull."

"What pull?" Alexei and Bryn asked in unison.

"The one from the brand," he sneered as if they were incompetent.

Cold dread pulled in Alexei's stomach. "How is that possible?"

"It isn't just a mark to expose someone. It tethers the person."

They had known where they were the whole time, following them, playing with them. He was one of the most powerful men in these lands and he'd had no idea. He thought of Clara and Kellen, but realized they must have found a way around it by staying within the wards.

Bradan looked at him like a dead man who didn't care what he said and sent him a vile grin. "You'll never get to her in time."

Anger shot through Alexei, and he punched Bradan with every bit of strength he had. His fist landed square on the other man's jaw. The force of it sent his head careening back against the tree before his head rolled forward. He was unconscious. Alexei's gray eyes turned to stone and landed on Finn.

"If she doesn't make it home, you won't either," he promised before he turned around to look at Bryn's stunned face. He didn't say another word as he took off toward the stream.

If what the soldier claimed was true, Aines surely would have found her by now. Worry flooded him when she was nowhere in sight. He tried to yell for her but felt his throat clog, his chest tight. What if he didn't get to her in time? What if he didn't find her at all? On instinct he turned and followed what he hoped was the right direction toward Westrim.

~ ~ ~

Nausea swept through Ellery as she felt herself coming to. She realized she was being carried and not by Alexei. She could tell the difference in the feel of the person holding her, their scent. She tried to raise her head, but she was too weak. She opened her eyes to see where she was, who she was with, and even that was difficult, as it was too blurry to see anything clearly. She tried to find her breath, but her throat burned. Despite that, she pushed and tried to ask a question, but she wasn't sure her words were coherent.

Warm breath fanned Ellery's face and the now familiar voice she heard sent a chill down her spine. Her body may not have been cooperating, but her mind told her she needed to get away, not wanting to be at the mercy of the man holding her hostage.

"Thanks for joining me. That was quite the stunt you pulled back there. I have to admit I was impressed. You might have gotten away with it, too, if James hadn't come along." He stopped. "Speaking of James, he went to get the others. To spread the good news of your homecoming. We need to wait here for the others before we go."

"Where?" Her voice sounded hoarse and distant.

She closed her eyes again as he sat down still holding her. The movement made her sick. The burning of her throat hadn't subsided, and she lifted a shaky hand to grab at the canteen that he offered. She took a sip and was relieved that it soothed her throat. When she gained a bit of her strength back, she moved to get off his lap.

"I wouldn't do that if I were you." His voice was low with a hint of warning.

"Do what?"

"Try to escape."

"And where do you think I'm going to go?" she said hotly and glared at him.

He considered what she said and watched carefully as she sat herself up beside him and leaned her back against a tree.

"Where is Alexei?"

"Don't you worry your pretty little head about him," he said and reached over to trail the back of his fingers down her cheek, down to the curve of her shoulder and against the side of her breast. "I'll take good care of you."

Disgust rolled through her, and she tried to pull away from his touch, the quick movement bringing on a wave of dizziness. Whatever she had inhaled still wasn't out of her system. She looked over at Aines and saw cold, emotionless eyes looking back at her.

Emotionless as they were, they were still striking, like the rest of him. She couldn't help but think that it wasn't fair that someone so wicked was so incredibly beautiful. It was a reminder that beauty could mask an ugly truth. A man like that would do what he wanted to satisfy his own needs regardless of who he hurt along the way.

"What are you going to do with me?"

"I'm going to take you back home, by whatever means necessary." He gave her an assessing gaze. "I'm not sure what makes you so damn valuable. But we'll know soon enough." He looked around, waiting for someone. She assumed the rest of the soldiers that he had been traveling with. "When the rest of them get here, we can leave."

She should have been offended at the question of her value, but she had been wondering the same thing. Was Bryn right, what they all assumed, was it possibly true? Then her mind wandered back to Alexei. What she wouldn't do to see that quick grin, feel his arms locked around her safely. She couldn't think of much more because the residual effects of the chemical still drained her. She closed her eyes and felt herself drifting off, despite doing her best to fight it.

CHAPTER TWENTY-TWO

When Ellery wasn't at the stream, with nothing left behind but the towel, Alexei was hardly aware of anything going on around him. All rational thoughts had left his head. He felt like his sanity was just out of reach. All of his life he had been brought up to be disciplined, put together, and it was hanging by a thread.

He took his knife from his boot and kept it in one hand knowing that he might have to use it and feeling more than willing to do so. He was in such a rage and was so focused that he didn't hear someone coming up behind him before they latched onto his arm.

Alexei turned around sharply and pulled back his arm that held the knife, ready to plunge it into whoever was there. He saw Bryn back up immediately, wide-eyed with astonishment. His friend stared at him as if had gone mad, and maybe he had. Alexei was breathing heavily, and without a word he turned to keep going.

"Damnit, Alex. Listen to me." Bryn grabbed his arm again. Alexei stopped but his body practically vibrated. "When they came this morning, I acted like I was sleeping. There were two of them, and they were talking about taking Ellery back home. They broke off and decided to search for her separately and meet back up after to take her back to the castle."

Alexei was flooded with relief knowing that she was alive, and they would at least keep her that way until she got back to the kingdom. Then, who knows what they would do.

It left an uneasy feeling in him to know that she wasn't safe past that and wouldn't be until she was with him again. Maybe not even then.

"They couldn't have gotten that far," Bryn said and thought for a moment, trying to calculate things in his mind. "They aren't familiar with these woods, so they would need to take the most direct path. Going further off of that would be too much of a risk. Let's separate and cover as much ground as we can."

They both tore off in the direction Bryn motioned toward and hoped that they were right. They veered off from each other. Alexei tried to think how long it had been since she had gone to the stream that morning. He didn't want to think of things that they could have done to her in that amount of time. The way they handled her the other day pierced his mind, and once again, fear clutched his stomach.

As Alexei ran through the dense forest, he sensed something. He realized what he was detecting, what was brushing up against his senses. It was magic, and it was near. This awareness of magic was a feeling that he had become aware of the last few days because of Ellery. It was power that seemed to call out to him now, that drew him toward it even though something equally powerful was telling him to run in the other direction. There was something different in the magic that he was sensing, something dark.

As the darkness of it seemed to stroke his senses, he saw it. There was a large black wolf staring right at him. He could sense something more than magic in the wolf, an evilness that sent shivers down his spine. This was no ordinary wild animal.

He cautiously approached the creature, unsure of what it wanted. And it did in fact seem to want something from him. The wolf snarled, baring its sharp teeth as it circled him. But he stood his ground, determined not to show any weakness.

The way the beast stared at him so intently with eyes that seemed almost human caused the hairs on the back of Alexei's neck to stand on end. The magic that he had sensed just moments ago was emanating from it. He could feel it then, see it in the yellow eyes that seemed to pierce him. It growled low, and there was something feral in it. He could feel his heart racing as the adrenaline pumped through his veins.

The animal seemed to be entranced, sent on a mission. He knew that he couldn't back down. Something told him even if he ran the wolf would follow and keep following until only one of them was left standing. He would stay and fight. The wolf paused, studying him carefully and when it stilled Alexei noticed a gold medallion hanging from its neck. He didn't have to get closer to see that the brand marred into Ellery's hand, the very one that he had associated himself with his whole life, was stamped into the medallion.

Before he could think any more about the implication, it gathered itself and lunged for him. There was no doubt now. The animal was on the hunt, and he was the target. It charged so quickly that he wasn't able to do anything but prepare for it. It slammed into him, and he rolled, trying to free himself. But before he could, it clamped down on his arm. He grunted in pain and pushed it off, landing a fist into the wolf. He sprang to his feet. He remembered the knife in his boot, reached down for it and ran. He knew in seconds the wolf would be on his heels.

He rifled through what he knew about wolves, and naturally the facts regarding their big teeth and strong jaws which he could attest to from the screaming pain in his arm from the wolf's bite. They could outrun their prey and simply exhaust them before making the kill, so making a run for it wasn't going to work. Then he remembered a fact about them jumping, and how they can reach a high arc. He took his eyes off of the wolf for a second or two to look around and saw what he had been looking for.

There was a big rock jutting out of the ground. Perfect. He slowly started to back up in that direction. The wolf, never losing focus and following, as he almost walked around it and almost behind it, he saw with relief that it leapt up on the rock and looked down. He could have sworn there was a gleam of intelligence in his eye.

Before he could think twice, he steadied himself as the wolf snarled and jumped. At the same time he brought up his knife and plunged it into the beast's muscled chest, striking true. He threw the animal to the side and watched as the malice left his eyes. In its last moments it was just a wolf. The spell had left it. It had been a battle of kill or be killed. But still, Alexei felt guilt as he saw the animal in pain before the life inside it left. It had to be done.

Pain lanced threw him and he looked down at his arm. The shirt was torn, as was his skin. Blood flowed but was slowing. It hurt like hell, but it could have been a lot worse. He stood there for a few moments, his heart still racing from what had just happened before he sheathed his knife and kept going. Ellery needed him.

Someone had enchanted the animal and sent it to kill him, of that he was sure. Who would do such a thing remained a mystery.

~ ~ ~

Ellery must have drifted off for a couple minutes. When she woke up everything was finally clear. She went to move and realized that her wrists were bound in front of her. The more she tried to move, the more something cut into her wrists. Handcuffs.

Aines leveled a smirk at her. He was guarding her closely… a little too closely for her comfort. "We wouldn't want you to slip through our fingers again, would we?" He reached over and placed one finger under her chin. "Now that I have your attention, I should tell you how well you will be treated is dependent on how good of a girl you are."

She ignored his empty promise and thought of ways to escape, and what she would do if an opportune moment presented itself. Absently she was tugging at the cuffs, trying to see how tight they were.

"You are going to give yourself bruises."

She ignored him again. Her thoughts went to Alexei.

Was he searching for her? Was he worried, or relieved, deciding that she wasn't worth the effort after all?

He stood and looked down at her with a malicious grin before he reached down and grabbed her by the arm and pulled her to her feet. "Here they come. We can finally be on our way."

She heard footsteps on the forest floor and braced herself for the rest of his posse to arrive. The sounds became closer, and Aines smiled at her, knowing that they had succeeded.

"Hopefully they have your lovesick boyfriend with them, so we don't have to deal with him later."

The thought of them hurting Alexei made her heart beat rapidly. She knew at this point he wasn't a prince to them, but just another target. She wondered how that was possible. She looked down, and her gaze lingered on a rock in front of her. She didn't have time to overthink it. She quickly grasped it as firmly as she could with her hands still cuffed in front of her and swiftly stood. She used all of her strength and hit him in the back of the head. Aines stumbled and slumped to the ground. When she was positive he wasn't moving, she dropped the rock and checked his unconscious body for a key to free her hands. Before she could rifle through all of the pockets, she heard the movements coming quicker, louder.

She stood to run after hearing shouts in pursuit, but after a moment recognized a familiar voice calling her name. She stiffened. She heard it again, and this time she let out a small sob of relief. She looked in the direction of the noise and she saw a tall, lean form running toward her, his blonde hair windblown and eyes filled with an intensity that took her breath away. Her legs shook in a mix of fear and relief as she whispered his name.

Alexei reached her at the same time that Bryn reached Aines' unconscious body. She looked up into his face that was as pale as hers felt. He reached up with his good arm and touched her cheek, letting out a breath when his skin touched hers, as if he had been worried that she wasn't real.

"I can't believe you found me."

"Of course I did. We are going to get you out of here." He raised his hands to her face and ran them down her cheeks, her neck, shoulders, down her arms to assure himself that she wasn't hurt. That was when he realized she was in handcuffs.

"I'm fine," she said, trying to reassure him. Her breath caught as she saw his bloody arm. "Who did that to you?" Tears pricked at her eyes.

He dismissed the injury as if it were nothing. "Just a wild animal."

He was more interested in making sure she was okay. Eyes that had just held hers with endless concern, now turned on Aines' body with a lethal stare.

"Honestly, Alexei, I am fine."

"I can see that." He gave her a slight smile when he saw that she was in fact, fine. His little warrior who had been concerned about being a damsel in distress had single-handedly knocked one of his soldiers out cold. He opened his mouth again, but she would never know what he was going to say because he saw Aines moving out of the corner of his eye.

He motioned for Bryn to come to her. Alexei stood over him as if he had all the time in the world, even gave him the opportunity to stand up and get his bearings until Aines moved to run. Alexei lunged at him, and they both fell to the ground. It was hard for Ellery to see through the movements as they wrestled on the ground. Adrenaline must have pumped through Aines because he seemed to have gotten a second wind. They exchanged punches and for a moment Aines seemed to take the upper hand. He tried to stand until Alexei grabbed him by the ankle, tripping him. Crawling over to him he kept him down, rising up above him, he began punching him repeatedly. He looked completely unhinged in a way that she had never seen.

"Alexei," Ellery yelled. He was going to kill Aines. Not that it would be any great loss, but he wouldn't need that on his conscience.

He stopped when he heard her voice, his fist raised in the air. He looked down at the unconscious man beneath him and lowered his fists. After a quick search of Aines' pockets, he unearthed a key. He brought the key and unlocked the cuffs. She sighed in relief, and he grabbed her hands, bringing them up to cup his face as he turned and pressed a kiss to each.

His voice was low and hard. "Bryn would you mind tying Aines up with the rest of them until I get back. We need to get help bringing the others back, but with everything, I'm not sure who to ask, or if Carwyn is even safe. We will need to think closely about who we can trust before we make a move." Bryn nodded. They had crossed paths right after the incident with the wolf but there hadn't been any time for explanations. "I'll be back as soon as I can. I need to get her to safety first then we'll take care of the rest."

She heard the word we. That they would take care of it. Together. Her stomach clutched.

He held out the cuffs to Bryn. "You'll need these."

They discussed next steps for a moment because the other soldier still hadn't returned. Four were tied up, Aines was there, and that left one more. With luck they would be able to detain him on the way. Without any other choice they decided to head in different directions, but before he turned to the still unconscious Aines, Bryn walked to Ellery and stared down at her for a few moments before leaning down to press a kiss on her cheek.

"Don't be scared," said Bryn quietly. "Everything will be alright." It was reassuring to hear the words even if they weren't true. He couldn't possibly know how it all was going to end.

She stood on her toes and gave him a tight hug. "Goodbye and thank you for everything."

"I don't like goodbyes. How about, until we meet again," he said, but it caused a pang in her chest, wondering if she would ever see him again. But she gave him one last smile before turning to Alexei.

"What happened?" he asked. He had just wrapped a makeshift bandage around his arm.

She told him everything that had occurred. As she relayed the events he reached down and squeezed her hand. She seemed to fully come back to herself as she talked through things. He knew they weren't out of the woods yet, so to speak, but feeling the weight of her hand in his and seeing her visibly relax did him good. She asked what happened on his side, and it was his turn to tell her what had happened. He left out a few details, like what he saw on that medallion.

He thought of the medallion that shined in the light, what had been carved into it, and the implications he wasn't ready to deal with. What did it mean? That medallion along with the fact that the wolf had magic in it, magic that had been used to hunt him. He had a feeling it had been more than a message, and he got it loud and clear. He didn't want her caught up in the crosshairs. Who knows what would be sent after him next, or when. Until he figured it out, he couldn't put her in harm's way any more than she already was.

"I need to find Carwyn."

"Is everything okay?"

He laughed sarcastically, and then gave her a look with a raised eyebrow. Everything was somehow completely right and completely wrong at the same time.

"Not exactly."

"Okay." He watched as her brilliant mind started sifting through a million different things at once. "Do we turn around and go back now?"

"No, Ellery. I need to turn around and go."

"But…"

"Don't worry, I'm going to get you there first."

"You think I'm worried about whether or not I can figure it out. I have been figuring it out my whole life. I don't need you to figure it out for me. I just need…" She bit her bottom lip, clearly trying to hold back emotions that he wished he wasn't responsible for. "You."

He closed his eyes and tried to still his emotions.

"What's wrong?" she said tremulously.

"I can't go with you."

Chapter Twenty-Three

"You can't, or you won't."

"Both."

"Why are you doing this?"

"I don't want to do this," he yelled. She flinched and it crushed him. "I don't have a choice." He winced and rolled his shoulder, and she noticed the rip in his shirt and the flash of red. She realized it was fresh blood. She reached for it, and when her hand reached his arm it came back red.

Her breath caught. "Let me bandage this up again."

"It's fine. I'm fine."

He wasn't even sure how to explain what he saw. He had a hard time believing it himself, so how was he to explain it to her? What could he say?

"I would rather you tell me to mind my own business than lie to me." It's not like they had held much back to this point. Everything they were had been laid out bare in front of them the last few days. Nowhere to hide, but both had places to run and apparently it wasn't in the same direction.

"Something happened, something more than just a rogue wolf, but I'm not even entirely sure what I saw, or if I saw it right. It's like reality has become so distorted the last few days, and the only thing that feels real is you. I need to keep you safe."

"We can keep each other safe."

He shook his head, and the look he gave her didn't remind her of Alexei, it reminded her of a prince, a future king. There was no give in that look, nothing to show that he was going to budge. It would be pointless for her to push. His ruling was final.

Shock was written across her face. He could sense the hurt growing inside of her as she processed what he had said, and he wished more than anything that he didn't have to be the one that caused it. But he had made up his mind and couldn't change it.

"I hope you understand," he said softly.

She didn't want to, but she did. He was willing to risk it all for her, so she would risk it for him. "I'll go with you. Let me help."

He shook his head. "It isn't safe for you."

Dreams of being with him came crashing down. She was a liability to him, and she knew it. That thought tore at her. "Because I'm a liability."

He looked at her with a tenderness she hadn't seen before, and it threatened to crush her. "You are a lot of things, but you are not, and never will be, a liability." She looked away, not believing it despite what she saw in his eyes.

"Nothing means more to me than your safety." He turned her face back to his. "That doesn't make you a liability, it makes you loved."

She pushed his last word away, not wanting to give in to it because it completely and wholly devastated her. Tears pooled in her eyes, and she felt like her heart was being torn apart. As quickly as he had come into her life, he would leave just as fast. The first time he told her he loved her it was a gift, but this time it was a goodbye.

Fear and pain surrounded her, and she lashed out. "So that's it, you are going to make the decisions for the both of us? Although, I shouldn't be surprised. Isn't that what kings do? Make decisions for everyone else so no one has a choice but to bend to your will."

She knew before the words even left her lips that she was out of line. She knew he wasn't like that, and that his greatest fear was being an unworthy king. She had just thrown salt in that wound. She was mad and wanted her words to hit their mark, and when he flinched, she knew it did. She felt small, hurting him out of anger and frustration instead of just telling him how she really felt. She moved in front of him and looked into his eyes, willing him to understand her regret.

"I'm sorry," she whispered softly.

"Don't worry about it." He started walking and sounded distant.

She wasn't sure how long they walked like that, in a tense silence. It wasn't the companionable silence she was used to. The wind blew through the trees, rustling their leaves and creating at least some sort of sound to break up the silence. She stole glances at him, and he looked deep in thought. His expression betrayed no emotions, but she knew that she had to have hurt him. She couldn't take it anymore and reached out to him. But before her hand grabbed his she pulled it back, feeling like she didn't have the right to give or receive that comfort. Mercifully he stopped.

She forced herself to meet his eyes and kept her hands at her sides when she either wanted to wrap them around him or wring them in front of her. "I didn't mean it. Not a word of it."

"I know you didn't. That is my own insecurity, things I need to deal with. You aren't responsible for that. I just couldn't bear to have you think, even a little bit, that it was the truth." They started to walk again, and he let out a deep sigh. "But you were right. I didn't give you a choice in this. The answer was always to go, and I never once asked what you wanted."

"You have done everything possible to protect me. Not doing what was best for you even though you surely should have. The fact that you put your own safety aside to do what you thought was right, to protect someone regardless of your own personal cost, if that isn't the sign of a good ruler, I don't know what is."

He stared at her, as if not believing what she was saying. She hoped they would have more time to smooth things out, to return to the easy familiarity that they had established between them. Instead, when she turned forward, her body gave a quick jolt when she saw the clearing that she recognized from her dreams.

"We are close," she whispered with dread and reluctant curiosity.

They walked the rest of the way to the edge of the forest and lingered. She knew what lay ahead, a future without him. She couldn't be selfish. He needed to help his uncle. He needed to go home. While a part of her was relieved that she may finally get some answers, as she was sure they would find what they were looking for, at the same time she was steeped in dread knowing that those answers would tear them apart. It was a combustible combination.

She kept her eyes on the clearing she had traversed so many times in her dreams. Then she spoke to him. "No matter what happens, I want to thank you. I have felt more and experienced more in the last few days than I have in my entire life. I never thought to know anything like this outside of books and dreams, and my own imagination. It has been the adventure of a lifetime."

"Your adventure isn't over." She noted that he didn't say "their" adventure.

She looked at him and said softly, "I don't want to leave you."

A feeling of helplessness surrounded him like another layer of skin. He was the future king. He would have more power, more resources, than anyone else in the land. Everything he needed, except the one thing that he wanted. The look she gave him was painful, and he wanted to soothe it.

"We won't be apart, not forever. But for now, I need you to be safe. Then I need Carwyn, the kingdom, to be safe. So, when I find my way back to you, I'll never have to leave you again." Although inside she knew he shouldn't make that kind of promise, and she could tell from the way that he looked at her that he didn't believe it either.

He leaned down. She felt the warmth of his lips and the slow, gentle rhythm of their kiss. The moment was achingly sweet and wrapped in sadness. All too soon, he pulled away, leaving her feeling an emptiness that could only be filled with another kiss, another touch, another stolen moment. A place that could only be filled by him.

Even though she knew what she would see, her breath caught, and she completely stilled when the kingdom beyond came into view. The castle sat in the distance and seeing it struck a chord in her heart. Its majestic turrets, strong walls, and sprawling grounds were a sight to behold. At first glance, a sense of belonging swept through her. She had never felt like she had belonged anywhere. Except, she couldn't admit to herself right then, with Alexei. The last few days finally made sense, and the pieces of the puzzle slid into place. That sense of belonging gave her one of the most peaceful moments she had ever known. All that remained was to figure out why. The answers beckoned to her, made her heart beat faster, and the odd mix of fear and excitement swirled inside of her. The link she felt, the affinity, gave her strength, courage, and the power to take the next step.

Alexei's curiosity piqued and he followed her gaze. All he could see was lush green hills for miles. She seemed transfixed by something unseen. "What do you see?"

She looked at him with a steady flame of joy in her eyes. "Home." The truth of it rang through her.

Something skirted around the edges of her mind and tried to get in. She paused and waited as it seeped into her subconscious and latched on. She let out a small gasp as understanding dawned.

Something still separated her from the world just beyond. She couldn't see it, but she knew it was there. She could feel it inside and felt inexplicably drawn to it. She took a few steps, slower this time. She put her arm in the air to touch it, but stopped short when she felt the energy that radiated off of it. A barrier. The thought rang clearly through her mind now.

The closer she got, a strange sensation ran through her, and she felt a subtle energy radiating from it. Taking a deep breath, she skimmed her finger along the barrier, feeling a rush of power as a tingle spread up her arm. It was inviting, calling to her. At her touch the wall began shimmering and suddenly appeared in front of her made of pure light.

She could feel it practically pulling at her skin, urging her to keep going, to let it surround her. Slowly, so slowly she reached her arm out again and this time she put it through the barrier. It felt like a warm embrace, and she wanted so desperately to be wrapped up in the way it made her feel. Wanting to take the next step through it to reach whatever fate lay ahead of her…

"Wait," she said to herself, thinking of Alexei. She pulled her arm back and with it the warmth faded. She turned to him and saw the fear on his face as well as fascination and understanding. His gaze seared her and lingered on every detail of her being. She shivered under that all-encompassing look, feeling exposed and vulnerable but unable to look away. Eventually, he blinked slowly and let out a deep breath.

He spoke softly in an almost reverent tone. "You are amazing."

She stepped toward him. She wasn't sure why, maybe to comfort both of them, but he shook his head.

"It's okay," he said.

He was letting her go. The realization hit her. She wanted to beg him to change his mind, to go with her, but she knew better. He wouldn't have been the man she fell in love with so fast, so fiercely, if he didn't go back to his uncle when he was in trouble. And that was what it was: love. He had finally taught her broken heart how to love. Instead of saying that, she slowly turned back toward the barrier.

Alexei stepped up beside her and reached out with curiosity. His good arm hit against the barrier he could now see. It had been clear, like glass, but it was as hard and immovable as steel. Even though he knew the answer, he wanted to test a theory. He began to walk away, and every couple feet he reached his arm up again, being blocked every time.

Fumbling around for the right words, he turned back to her when a sudden movement alerted him. His gaze quickly shot to the bank that they had walked down from, and he saw a soldier cresting the hill, but the man wasn't looking at him. His gaze was set in stone on Ellery. Fear clawed and spread as he darted forward and watched as the soldier raised his gun. As he cocked it, Alexei reached Ellery, using his speed to propel them both to the ground as he covered her body with his own.

He felt something rip into his side. Pain seemed to tear through the skin and plunge itself deep into him.

Chapter Twenty-Four

The pain that tore through his body was unlike anything he had ever felt before. She started to move beneath him.

"Hold on. Not yet." He kept himself over her, worrying that another shot would be taken, although it pained him to move. He turned his head and looked up to where the soldier had been and saw that he was gone.

He scanned the rest of the hill and saw no one. She was still trying to wiggle out from underneath him, and he rolled to the side and began to search her for injuries. He was filled with relief when he saw that she was unharmed. "Are you okay?"

"Besides the bruise I'm going to get on my hip from the fall, I'm fine." She went to ask him what the hell he had been thinking until she saw his face creased with something more than concern. It was pain.

At that moment Alexei felt the warm blood as it trickled down his shirt, cooling when it mixed with the air. He reached down to feel what he already knew, that he had been shot.

Ellery screamed as she saw the bright red blood against his shirt. She reached for him, and he grabbed her hand, shaking his head. Even though he was panting from the pain and trying to catch his breath, when he spoke, he spoke as calmly as he could. "I'm fine."

"What happened?" She reached for him again, his shirt damp from blood and sweat.

"It was a soldier. He is gone, but he won't be the last. You need to go now."

He could feel the pain begin to cloud his thoughts, growing more intense with each passing moment. He knew he needed to get her to safety before it became too much to bear. She couldn't be left at the mercy of whoever might crest that hill next. That thought was more terrifying than anything else. He tried to shift and gasped for breath as the blast of pain surged through him. He tried to focus on anything but the throbbing agony that felt like a vise on his side. His vision began to blur, and he felt himself slipping away as he drifted into oblivion.

Ellery's heart raced, and her breath came in short gasps. Fear had taken over, pushing away any rational thought she might have had. The cold grip of fear seemed everywhere, pressed in on all sides of her without escape. Her old acquaintance, helplessness, started to trickle in. She fought back against the feeling that had so often consumed her in the past and channeled those raw and exposed feelings, and when she did, something swelled inside of her. She felt it grow and expand until she thought she would burst.

Power.

It tingled throughout her body like a million tiny sparks. She looked down at her suddenly warm hands, and her breath hitched as the light seemed to mold itself to her, all of her, as if it emanated from her body.

The familiar surge of energy multiplied within her with each passing second, consuming her, wholly focused on the man laying at her feet. Grief, sharp and strong, gripped her just as strongly and threatened to erupt inside. It was like a force that had been lying dormant. It was as if her grief and desperation for Alexei, so deep, so encompassing, had awoken something within. The air was filled with mystical energy that shook the ground beneath her and stirred up a fierce wind. It rose and fell inside her like an invisible sea before it shot outward in a powerful current. She was so saturated in fear, so focused on Alexei, that she didn't see that as she sobbed the power shot out of her in a wave. That wave had a target she didn't consciously choose. The soldier who had shot Alexei crested the hill again but collapsed when the wave of energy blew through him.

When the wind subsided, and the ground stilled, the brightness of the light dissipated and settled into a steady glow. There was a moment of stillness so intense that all sound ceased except her breathing. It was as though she had been living in a fog, and now it had cleared, giving way to clarity and understanding. She looked around and saw that everything around her appeared brighter and more vivid than ever before, almost magical in its beauty. Although the most beautiful thing to her, the most precious, was who lay before her.

When Alexei woke moments later, he realized he was still lying on the cold ground. He opened his eyes and squinted against an overpowering brightness, shielding his eyes with a hand. For a moment, he could only make out an intense white light. As the brightness of it began to dim and his eyes adjusted, a figure appeared above him in the middle of the bright expanse. With a start he realized it was Ellery, and his breath caught in his throat.

A radiant hue spread across every inch of her skin and set her body alight. She hovered over him, tears sliding down her face, and all he could think was that she looked like she was made of starlight.

Despite the turmoil inside of her, her voice was gentle and soothing when she spoke to him. "Stay still. Let me take a look."

She knew she had to get him somewhere safe, but her head spun. She took a deep breath and, focused, reached out. He winced in pain as she carefully peeled his shirt away from the wound. She could see that it was deep and bleeding but wondered if somehow it had avoided any major organs or arteries since he was still alive. She turned to reach for the pack for something to apply pressure to the wound, and before she could, his hand came up to cup her cheek, and his thumb ran gently across to wipe away the tears.

"Ellery."

"Shh." She brought her hand up to cover his.

"You'll be fine. You'll be safe," he said as if reassuring himself. Although the pain threatened to devour him, he didn't care if it swallowed him whole as long as she was safe first.

"I won't leave you," she said as panic filled her at the thought, worrying she would never see him again. She needed to get him to safety. "I won't," she said again, stubbornly, and he could see her start to panic. "Let's go somewhere safe. We belong together!" Her voice grew desperate.

He gave her a look of resignation and nodded his head before he used the strength he had left to pull himself to his feet. Relief passed through her when she realized that he was going to take her with him. He was in too much pain to put up a fight. They would figure it out together, and once he was healed, they would make things right.

He cupped her face and kissed her quickly, pouring all his heart into it, not leaving room for any doubt of what he felt for her and what she meant to him.

With a muted grimace of pain, he lowered his hands down her face to her arms as if to pull her into an embrace.

But instead of the embrace, he whispered in her ear, "I love you. Wherever you are, whatever world you are in, I will find you."

He gripped her arms and used the last of his strength to push her. He watched her bewildered eyes stared into his as she fell backward through the invisible barrier. When he saw her body disappear, a relief like he had never known flooded through him realizing that she was safe. Then Alexei collapsed.

EPILOGUE

Three days later...

The sounds of the lecture hall merged together to become one melody of chaos. She heard a cacophony of conversations, laughter, shuffling of feet and chairs, and pens scratching against paper. Ellery found comfort in the noises. They reminded her of who she was, and why she was there. A few days before, she had woken up feeling that some part of her was somehow detached. Ever since, she had been going through the motions and tried her best to ignore it, but the feeling kept resurfacing within her. She felt uneasy and disoriented, and there seemed to be no remedy for what was happening inside her.

She had a class that morning and had just arrived a few minutes before. The lecture hall was massive. It was one of the biggest on campus. A single podium stood at the front of the room, a comforting reminder to everyone gathered that someone seemingly had it all figured out. The ceiling stretched high, and from every corner of the dimly lit space, one could hear the chatter of students as they shared their thoughts and ideas before the class began. She had sat in this hall many times before while the professor's voice echoed off the walls as he lectured enthusiastically, making it hard for anyone not to be engaged. Over the last year, it was a place that wasn't just a room filled with desks and chairs, it was a sacred place to her, and still, she felt disconnected.

The professor hadn't yet arrived, and there remained a feeling of anticipation as each student ensured they found a seat and what they needed for class. Laptops and notebooks littered every surface, prepared to partake in whatever knowledge would be imparted to them. Ellery had sat towards the back and pulled her stuff out of her bag. She pulled out the first thing her hand closed around. She smiled when she pulled out the young adult book she had borrowed from the library at Lily's sterling recommendation, hoping it would ease whatever was going on inside her as many books usually did.

She looked down at the cover. It was black with dark green vines crawling around the edges, and in the background sat an imposing castle. The picture it made was beautiful. The vines snaked around to the back as she followed them and turned it over to read the back cover. The synopsis promised that a world full of enchanted creatures, unimaginable powers, and fated love waited inside. She turned the book back around, slid her hand over the cover, and stopped to trace the embossed gold title with the tip of her pointer finger. When she reached the word fate, her heart raced as the letters seemed to pulse under her touch.

Fate.

The word rang through her head. It dug and clung to her like there was some importance attached to it that she couldn't remember.

Just then, the professor strode into the room, curbing her thoughts. He laid his laptop on the desk before heading to the podium to speak to them. Before he could, another man entered the room, and she heard murmurs and a few delighted giggles. She took a good look, and she was sure she had never seen him, yet he seemed strangely familiar. He had a mysterious air around him. He wore a suit that looked to have been tailored specifically for the lean lines of his tall body. The slate gray color of the suit looked striking against his dark brown hair. She studied the rest of his face and took in the beard that was closely clipped around his mouth so carefully, as though his lips were a painting in a frame… she couldn't deny the masterpiece. She sat straighter in her seat as if she could get a better look at the mysterious and alluring visitor.

Her professor called out to the class, "We have a surprise visitor today. I want everyone to welcome Dr. Sonders. He is a visiting lecturer and has been kind enough to take a look at your theses."

Sonders. The name caused some strange feeling to crash over her. Something tried to push through her mind to the point that it created a sheen of sweat on her face. As if the emotions were coming off her in waves, the namesake looked up alertly. Although there had to have been at least one hundred students in the class, his eyes found hers and held. Her breath caught in her throat, and time slowed as she held his gaze. Keeping his eyes on hers, he stepped forward, and her chest tightened like something compelled him to move closer. She felt it too, and anticipation filled up inside of her.

A chair was pulled out and scraped across the floor, breaking the moment between them. Dr. Sonders shook his head as if clearing it from the trance he had been in before he cleared his throat and turned to the rest of the class.

"Thank you so much for having me today."

He continued to speak after he wrote his topic on the board. He lectured for the rest of the class, never meeting her gaze again.

Though the moment passed, the feeling stayed with her, lurking in her mind like an unwelcome guest. She tried to ignore it and concentrate, and finally, at the end of class, she picked up her bag and fought the urge to run. She felt stifled and hot. She was so deep in her own thoughts she didn't hear anyone come up behind her.

She felt a light pressure on her elbow and when she jumped, she dropped everything in her hands with a loud clatter. She had been in such a hurry to get out she hadn't put her things back in her bag. She turned around and watched as Dr. Sonders put his hands up in surrender before dropping down to retrieve the items she had dropped. The breath she held from the gasp refused to exhale when she took in the man before her. She had to actively force herself to breathe.

"I'm sorry," he said, looking up at her with a soft smile. "I didn't mean to scare you."

She returned the smile and dropped beside him, forgetting what she was doing because her hands froze. She tried not to let her gaze linger too long, but when their eyes met, something seemed to pass between them and held tight. For days she'd felt like the world around her had been spinning out of control. But with just one look, he had grounded her to that moment.

Like his hair, his eyes were the darkest brown that she had ever seen, they almost looked black. Like the midnight sky without stars, yet far from empty… it was a shade that reminded you of the potent color held in every beam of the rainbow. She could certainly get lost in their wonder if she dared let herself explore. His dark hair was clipped shorter, but long enough that she could run her fingers through it. The thought made her cheeks burn even more. As he no doubt took in her flushed face, those eyes sparkled with amusement, and his perfect white teeth flashed in a smile. His smile only emphasized the curve of his jawline. His sharp features were bracing.

When they stood, he handed over her stuff and put his hands in his pockets, cutting a casual stance. Even as he appeared relaxed, something about his demeanor betrayed him. His presence commanded attention, and she couldn't help but give it to him. It felt like she had met him before, or that she had felt this way before. How could a stranger feel so familiar? The weight of his stare on her made every nerve ending seem to be on fire.

The two stayed there for a few moments longer before she broke the silence with a nervous laugh. "Thank you for your help. I'm sorry, I'm all out of sorts today." She put everything in her bag before looking back at him.

She was unsettled to see that he was looking at her expectantly, like he was willing her to remember something. She could feel her heart pounding as he stepped closer and extended his hand. For a brief moment, she hesitated before reaching out and grasping his.

His hand felt warm and firm around hers. "Have we met before?" she asked.

"Regrettably, no."

His lips twitched. She would have loved to know what he was thinking.

"I asked your professor to point you out at the end of class. I was able to read through your thesis. Your work is very impressive." He moved aside as the rest of the students filed out, and she realized with a start that they were now the only two left in the room. "That kind of writing takes a lot of talent and passion about the topic, and it shows."

"Thank you." She looked closer for mockery but saw none.

"Where do you get your inspiration?" He leaned back against the nearest desk and grasped the edge.

"Dreams," she said without thinking. She felt her face flush as soon as the word escaped her mouth. Embarrassment washed over her. She couldn't believe she had just said that out loud. It sounded crazy.

At her answer, one side of his mouth curved upward. "What interesting dreams you have, Ms. Faidman."

"Ellery," she said.

"Ellery." He repeated her name as if he liked the way it sounded. "Your ability to craft characters and set scenes in such vivid detail is a gift." Then he stared at her pointedly. "You have an uncanny ability to take your reader there, as if you have walked the lands of that distant realm yourself."

Her face lit up at the thought. "Wouldn't that be incredible?" She thought of the dream world that she had inhabited for months, and how exhilarating it would be to visit.

He pushed off the desk and walked toward her, only stopping when he was close, too close. She had to fight the urge to step back. "What if I told you that the possibility isn't as out of reach as you may think?"

She laughed at the absurdity of what he had just said but quickly stopped when she saw the seriousness of his expression. Her tone softened. "I'm sorry. I didn't mean to offend you. It's just... what you're saying isn't possible." She tried to give him a look that indicated it was obvious why.

She thought of all the books she had read over the years and how desperately she wished she could have escaped into any one of them and left her life behind. She searched his face for an answer as to why he thought such a thing would be in the realm of possibility.

He steeled her with a look that was full of determination and promise. "Humor me for a moment."

"Okay." She nodded slowly, trying to absorb the whole of the last five minutes.

"Let's assume I could take you there. To that land of your dreams, that world you have brought to life with your clever words. Would you want to go with me?"

"More than anything," she said automatically and meant it. "What an incredible gift that would be."

She thought of how extraordinary it would be to walk through the world that had taken up so much space in her head, her dreams, pulling on every bit of her imagination. Her mind was so far off that she was startled when he reached for her bag and laid it on the desk beside her, but she didn't move.

Then he turned back to her, grasped her hand, and pulled it to his lips. "Then let this be my gift to you," he said.

Before she could tell him he had completely lost it, she felt a warmth envelop her as his lips brushed against her skin. Her body went rigid as memories flooded back raw and powerful. Her panicked gaze met his as emotions threatened to drown her. Fear, anticipation, excitement, desire, wonder, and a whole other spectrum of feelings saturated her.

She took a deep breath and tried to bring the memories to the forefront, but she quickly realized that they were fragments, smaller pieces of a whole. It was like seeing pictures and short reels but only part of the film. Because of that, she couldn't attach all of the emotions that had flooded her with the memories they belonged to.

It was like two halves of a whole that she couldn't put back together. The force of it left her breathless and threatened to bring her to her knees. The missing pieces left her with jagged edges inside that made her ache. But even with the ache, she felt real, felt whole, for the first time in days.

"It is real. All of it," she stammered.

He nodded, his gaze searching hers. She tried to pull at the memories that floated around, desperately trying to fit them all together. While a few were whole, some just came and went in flashes. She tried to push for more, the desire for it so strong that she caught herself wavering a bit, and he reached out to steady her.

"Don't push it." His voice was low and soothing.

"Alexei," she breathed in a panic as a blood-stained shirt entered her mind. She tried to steady her hand as it trembled.

Although he looked at her with concern, he nodded in encouragement. "What do you remember?" he murmured.

"Bits and pieces. It is like fragments of memories, only a few complete." She remembered the first moment she saw Alexei when he saved her at the river. A kiss, she thought and slowly raised her fingers to her lips, and finally she pulled out the piece of memory again where there was blood all over him. "He's hurt."

"That's why I'm here. I need your help. My name is Carwyn. I'm–"

She spoke in a breathless whisper. "Alexei's uncle."

Another memory hit her, remembering he was the king. Was she supposed to curtsy? She moved to do so, and he reached out and grasped her upper arm, pulling her up and just a bit closer to him. "Just Carwyn, Ellery."

"Carwyn." She repeated his name as he had hers, and he gave her an odd look as it left her mouth. She tried to decipher the look, but it was already gone.

"Alexei is missing," he said.

She felt like there was more to that statement, but she couldn't think of it.

"I thought you could help." His voice was low and urgent.

"What happened?"

Again, she tried to push her brain. For the first time she looked at his chest and a pin with the emblem of wolf standing tall stared back at her. She had seen it before. It was an answer to another question she didn't know.

"There were reports of him being hurt, but he was gone by the time we got to him. I was hoping you could help us find him. Do you remember anything about it?"

She didn't. She pushed against whatever mental block held her back again, trying to will the memories. Her head began to pound from the effort.

He must have seen it because he reached out and brushed a finger across her temple. "You are going to give yourself a headache. They will come with time. Be patient."

"Why was he hurt? Was it because of me? Because he helped me? But why, that doesn't make sense?" Why had he been helping her in the first place? She was starting to spiral, and he reached out a hand to clasp one of her shaking hands, keeping it in his.

"Ellery," he said quietly. "Don't be scared. I will keep you safe."

Her anxiety rose as the reality of the situation dawned on her. He seemed aware of her thoughts and feelings, giving her the space she needed to comprehend things, his gaze never wavering. She felt unable to process what was happening around her.

At that moment, she could only look at him and try to make sense of the confusion clouding her mind. Her brain ached with fatigue. She felt like there was something else she should remember about him, about everything, but all she could remember was how much Alexei loved him and the respect he had for him as a ruler. Alexei had been proud of him.

"I'm not asking you to trust me. I'm asking you to trust my nephew."

From the pieces of memories she had, she knew she did. Alexei had saved her, and now it was time for her to save him.

She braced herself for what would come next and nodded slowly before addressing him. "I do trust him."

"You'll go with me?" he repeated as if trying to make sure he heard her correctly.

Ellery nodded before she could change her mind. He gave her a look that gleamed with satisfaction before he put his arm around her and pulled her to him.

"Hold on tight."

He looked down and smiled and in the next moment, the lecture hall was like a distant memory, transformed into the world she'd come to know, come to love.